COSMO FAMILIA*
01
Presented by HANOKAGE

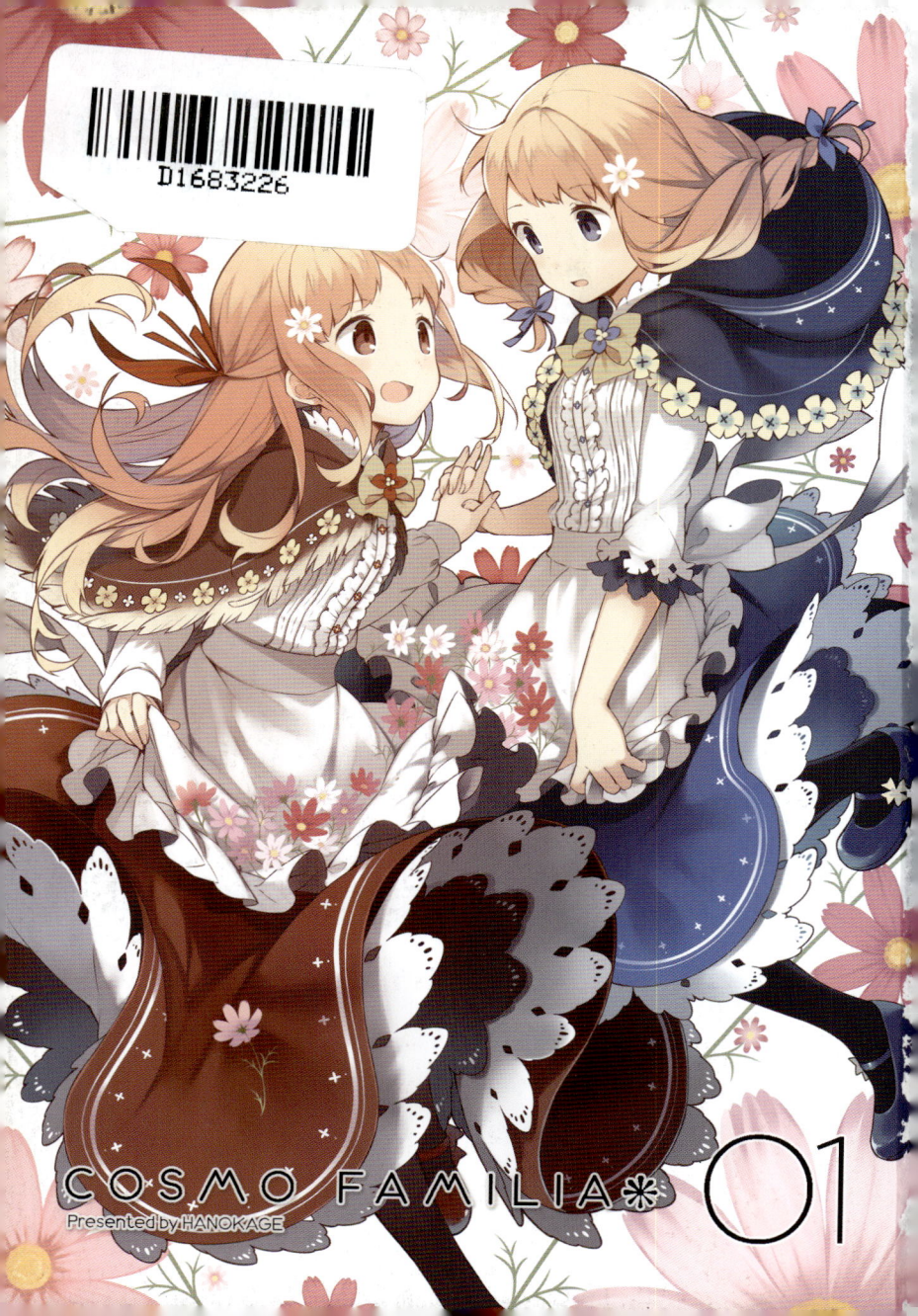

CONTENTS

Cosmo Familia Vol. 01
Presented by HANOKAGE

Chapter 01	Birthday	003
Chapter 02	Cosmof	039
Chapter 03	Alice	067
Chapter 04	Raika	095
Chapter 05	Rain	119
Chapter 06	Night	135
Chapter 07	Transform	151

HOUSE-SIT?
YES! CAN YOU HOUSE-SIT LIKE A GOOD GIRL?
Heh heh. I WONDER IF SHE CAN MANAGE IT. ALICE-SAMA IS STILL QUITE THE BABY, SO...
I AM NOT!
I'M ALREADY TEN YEARS OLD, YOU KNOW!
THE COSMOFS AND PAPII ARE HERE TOO, SO IT'LL BE EASY-PEASY!
OKAY, I GET IT! I'LL LEAVE THE HOUSE-SITTING TO YOU, ALICE!
I'M ON IT!
SO, PLEASE COME HOME SOON, IMORI... MOTHER-SAMA...
HAPPY BIRTHDAY, ALICE-CHAN!

HAPPY SIXTEENTH BIRTHDAY!!
......
SI...LENCE...
YEAH, RIGHT!
RE-ALLY...
SIX YEARS AND NOT A PEEP!
COME HOME ALREADY! REEEE-AAAALLY!!
Waaaah...

Chapter 01 Birthday

OKAY! I'M GOING TO EAT THIS BIRTHDAY CAKE!
SQUEEE!
THIS IS DELICIOUS...!
NICE TO MEET YOU.
munch
munch
I'M AMAKAWA ALICE.
I JUST TURNED SIXTEEN TODAY.
I'M ACTUALLY EATING BREAD... I MISS IMORI'S CAKES AND GOURMET MEALS.
MY FAMILY'S MADE UP OF ME, MY MOTHER, AND OUR ONE SERVANT.
EVERYONE EXCEPT ME HAS BEEN GONE FOR SIX YEARS.
BEEP
BEEEP
RIGHT NOW, ONLY ME...
WARNING!
!!
AND MY MOM'S "PETS" LIVE IN THIS HOUSE.
INTRUDER ALERT!
SO, THEY'RE HERE, HUH?

TP TP
TP...
KA-SLAM
I'VE SPENT THESE PAST SIX YEARS ALONE...
JUST WAITING FOR EVERYONE TO COME HOME.
GAAAH!
WHOO
WOOSH
I AM "HOUSE-SITTING LIKE A GOOD GIRL."
HEEEEY!

BOOOM!!
SKIIID
mosh!
THIS HOUSE ...
POP
THUMP
IS NOT YOUR FOOD!
THUMP
THUMP
HOW MANY TIMES DO I HAVE TO TELL YOU THIS, AL-READY ?!!
FLASH
ROAR!!!

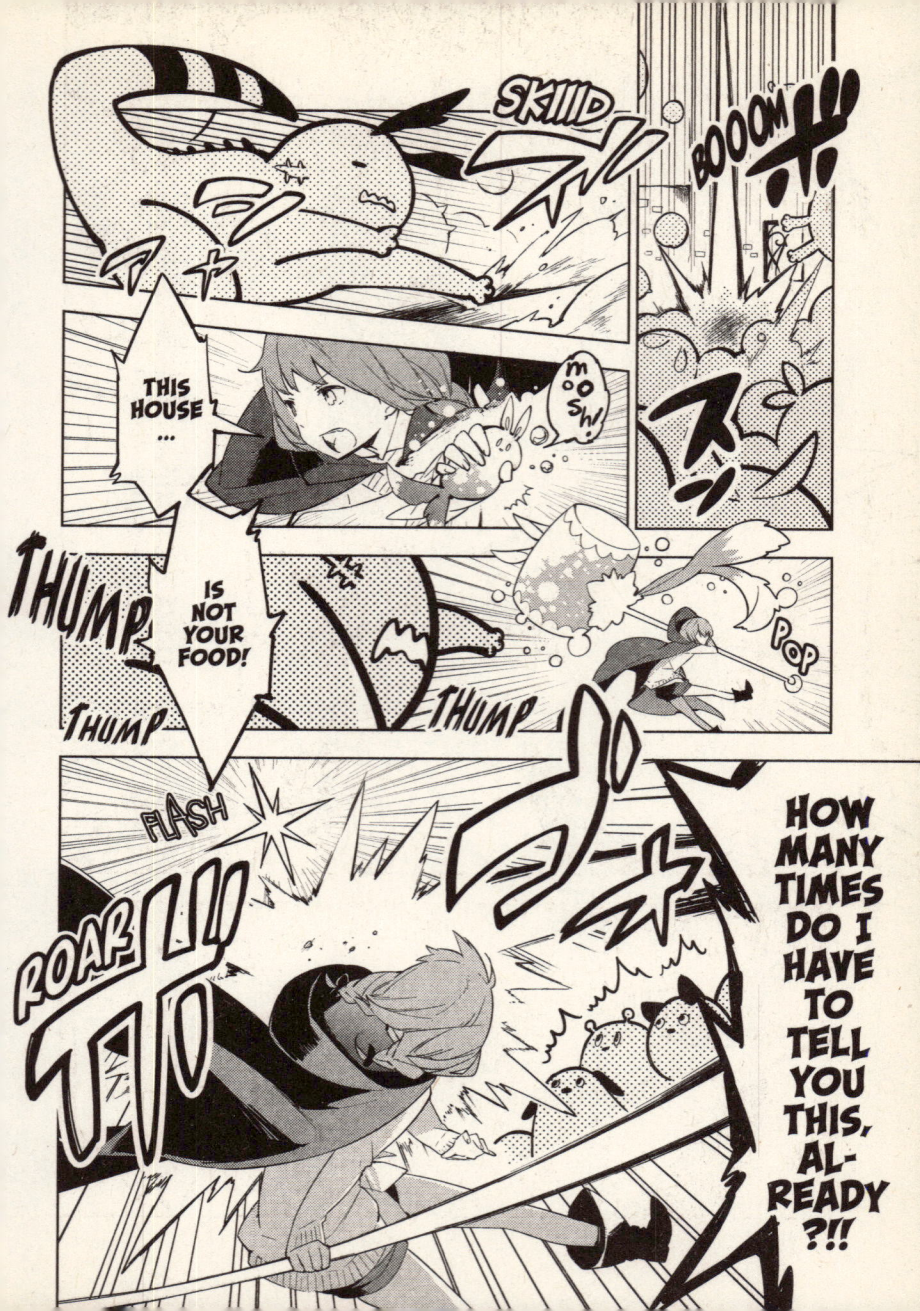

FWOOSH...
アッ...
BANG
GOT IT?!
IT DOESN'T MATTER HOW MANY TIMES YOU SHOW UP!
YOUR OWNER IS NOT HERE!!
FLINCH
...
SO HURRY ON BACK TO YOUR NESTS!
DROOP...
TRUDGE
TRUDGE...

......
THEY'RE FINALLY GONE.
BONK
REALLY! EVERY SINGLE NIGHT--
OW...!
MUNCHA
MUNCHA
WHAAAAAT?!
CRUNCH
CRACK
CRACK SMASH
CRACK
TH-THE ROOF...
THAT HORRIBLE SOUND IS...
YOOUU...
FLAP...
FLAP...
STUPID COS-MOOOFS!
THESE STRANGE CREATURES...

SETTLED IN THIS TOWN ABOUT TWENTY YEARS AGO.
THEY'RE CALLED COSMOFS.
I GUESS YOU COULD SAY THAT THEY'RE BASICALLY "ALIENS"...
BUT IF YOU WANT TO PUT A NEGATIVE SPIN ON IT, THEY'RE...
Ngh...! THEY SURE MADE A HUGE MESS WHILE THEY ATE.
HOW AM I GOING TO FIX THIS...?
DESTRUCTIVE INVADERS FROM OUTER SPACE!
SHUOOO

PAPII, WHAT ARE THE CHANCES FOR RAIN FOR THIS WEEK?
THERE IS A THIRTY TO SIXTY PERCENT PROB-ABILITY OF CLOUDI-NESS WITH A CHANCE OF COS-MOFS.
IT MAY BE NECESSARY TO SEND OUT A COSMOF ALERT TO THE TOWN.
GUESS I BETTER HEAD DOWN TO TOWN, THEN.
ALSO, THE BOILER HAS BEEN DAMAGED AND MAY REQUIRE REPAIRS.
WHAT? BUT I JUST FIXED IT.
IT WAS DAMAGED JUST NOW BY THE COS-MOFS.
WHAT?!
STUPID! STUPID! IDIOTIC PESTS!
YOU'VE GOT A WEIRD NAME! DON'T COME BACK AGAIN!
AND YOU'D BETTER PAY ME FOR THE DAMAGES!!!
OH, ALICE. THE COSMOFS ARE PART OF OUR FAMILY AS WELL.
RAIKA WILL SCOLD YOU FOR SPEAKING ILL OF THEM.
Humph... SO, YOU'RE ON *THEIR* SIDE THEN, PAPII?
....

I KNOW.
IT'S NOT ALL THEIR FAULT.
PAPII...
AM I REALLY A BAD GIRL?
IS THAT WHY IMORI AND MOTHER-SAMA...
WON'T COME HOME?
LOW BATTERY. ENTERING SLEEP MODE.
REPLY FUNCTIONALITY TERMINATED.
Huh?!
HEY!
SIGH...
I SHOULD JUST GO TO SLEEP MYSELF.
THIS IS MY FAMILY.
THIS IS THE AMAKAWA FAMILY, WHO'VE MADE ENEMIES OF EVERYONE UNDER THE STARS.

REQUEST FOR REPAIRS? BROKEN SOMETHING AGAIN?
I DIDN'T BREAK IT, *THEY* BROKE IT.
I'll only give you enough to get by.
OH, AND DO YOU HAVE ANY CANDY?
TODAY'S MY BIRTH-DAY, BUT...
HUH?
OF COURSE WE DON'T HAVE THOSE KINDS OF LUXURIES.
"THEY'VE" GONE WILD AGAIN AND OUR SUPPLIERS ARE LATE.
KANG KANG
So it's canned goods for all of us.
WHAT?
I'm so tired of this.
HARDTACK
AND WHO'S THE ONE WHO CHASES "THEM" OFF?
MAYBE MY LOW BLOOD SUGAR WILL **SLOW ME DOWN** WHEN YOU NEED ME TO MOVE.
OH, FOR...!
TOSS
HERE!
!

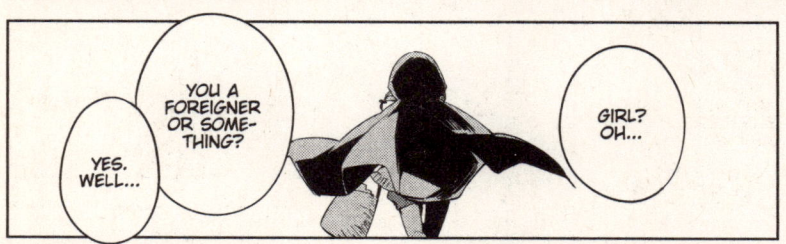

THANKS, YOU SUPER-STINGY HA-- STORE-KEEPER!
YOU WERE ABOUT TO CALL ME A "HAG," WEREN'T YOU?!
See you later!
REALLY...! OH, A CUS-TOMER! WEL-COME!
WE DON'T HAVE MUCH IN STOCK RIGHT NOW. I'M SO SORRY FOR THE INCON-VENIENCE, BUT--
EXCUSE ME, I'M HERE FOR SOMETHING ELSE. I WOULD LIKE TO ASK ABOUT...
SWF...
THAT YOUNG GIRL A MOMENT AGO. DID SHE DO SOME-THING?
GIRL? OH...
YOU A FOREIGNER OR SOME-THING?
YES. WELL...
GLANCE
I SEE. SORRY. OUR TOWN IS PRETTY BORING.
Oh---...
THE AMAKAWA FAMILY, THOUGH-- EVEN FOR-EIGNERS MUST HAVE HEARD OF THEM, NO?
THE RUMORS SAY THAT IT WAS **AMAKAWA RAIKA** WHO BROUGHT THE VERMIN AND THEIR RAMPAGE.
THAT KID'S HER DAUGHTER.

THE TOWNSPEOPLE GIVE HER THE COLD SHOULDER.
WE ALL KNOW IT'S NOT HER FAULT...
BUT, WELL...THE DAMAGE WAS REALLY BAD AROUND HERE, SO...
This just in. A designated World Heritage Site...
was attacked by the things known as Cosmofs, and the damage...
AM FM
"DAMAGE," YOU SAY, BUT IT SEEMS MORE LIKE...
YOUR BASIC WEAR AND TEAR.
WELL, THAT'S BECAUSE WE HAVE COMPETENT SECURITY.
AND THAT IS...?
THE AMAKAWA GIRL HUNTS THE COSMOFS.
IRONIC, ISN'T IT?
WE DEPEND ON AN AMAKAWA TO PROTECT OUR DAILY LIVES.
Ha ha ha!
......

IT SEEMS THE RUMORS WERE TRUE.
THANK YOU. Please keep the change.
Thank you for your business!
OH DEAR. YOU DIDN'T ACTUALLY BUY ANYTHING JUST NOW, DID YOU?
What is this, anyway?
COMPENSATION FOR THE INFORMATION YOU PROVIDED.
Gold..?
INFOR-- WHAT?
WHO ARE YOU...?
A MEMBER OF THE INTER-GALACTIC POLICE FORCE.
BEAM
CLACK
CLACK
I- INTER-GALACTIC ...?
Mama, that person's wearing funny clothes.
WHAAAT ...?
It's not polite to stare!
......
I THINK I COULD USE THIS.

PERFECT! THE BEAMS THAT THE RAIN GOT TO WERE ROTTEN...
BUT IT LOOKS LIKE THE WOOD INSIDE IS STILL GOOD!
ALICE, I MUST CAUTION YOU.
THIS MAY BE CONSIDERED TRESPASSING AND THEFT.
NO ONE COMES AROUND HERE ANYMORE, SO IT'S ALL RIGHT. IT'LL BE FINE.
STILL...
THIS MUST HAVE BEEN AN AMAZING BUILDING, HUH?
WASN'T IT A SCHOOL BEFORE IT GOT TRASHED?
RECORDS SAY IT WAS...**OUGI ACADEMY,** A PRIVATE HIGH SCHOOL FOR GIRLS.
Hmm...
IF **THEY** HADN'T RUN WILD...
THEN I MIGHT HAVE GONE SOMEWHERE LIKE THIS.

BAM
WARNING! RADIUS THREE KILOMETERS!
COSMOF ACTIVITY DETECTED!!
BOOOOM
THUD
PWOOOO!
THUD
THUD
THUD
ONE LARGE COSMOF SIGHTED.
IT IS HEADED FOR THE OPPOSITE SIDE OF TOWN. WHAT WILL YOU DO, ALICE?
WE DON'T HAVE TO BOTHER WITH IT, THEN. LET'S JUST KEEP AN EYE ON IT, AND...
LIKE...
WAIT! WAIT A MINUTE, PAPII-- OVER THERE!!
THUD

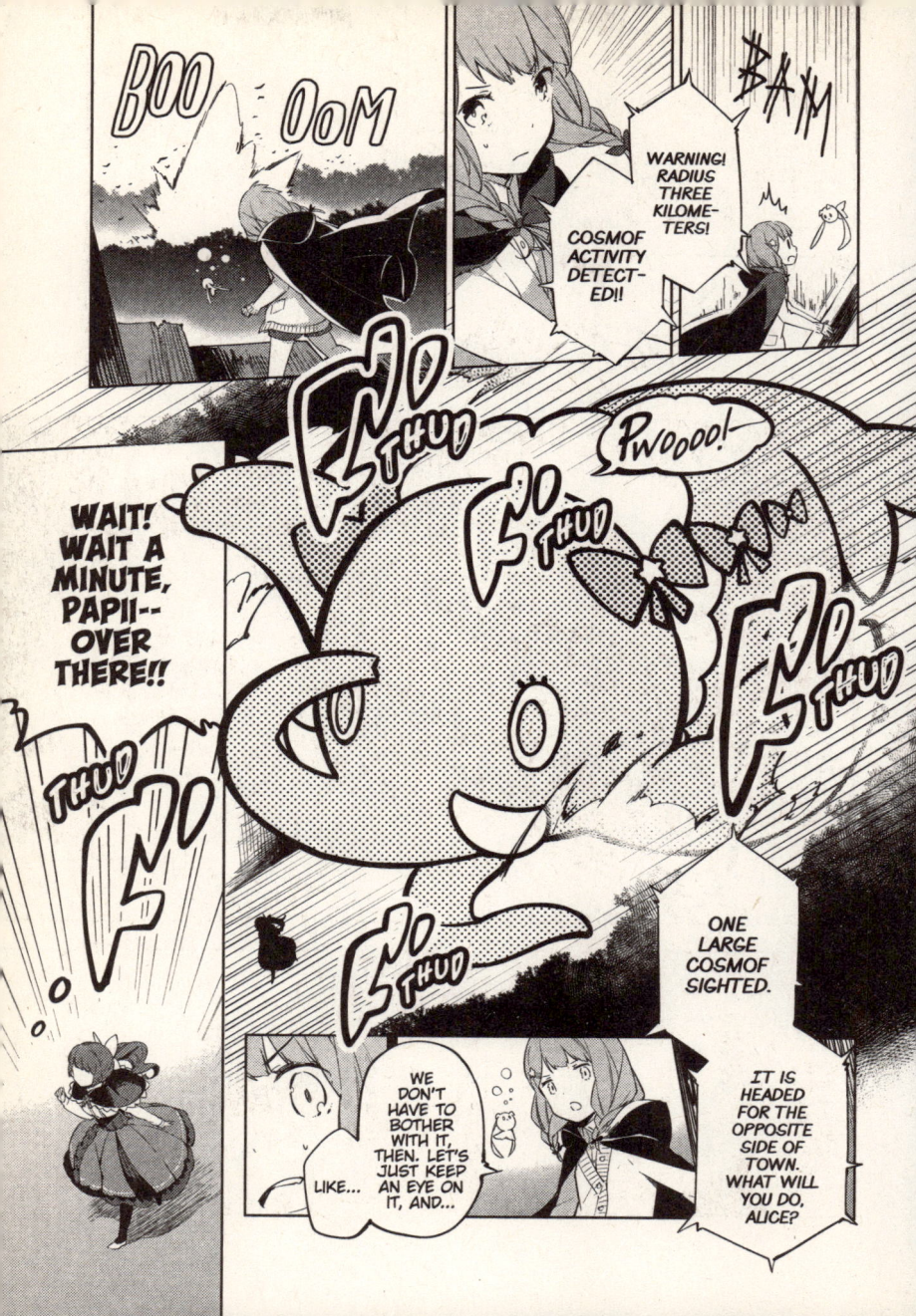

PATTER PATTER
Huff!
Huff...!
SMACK
Eek ?!
THUDD
THUDD
WHUMP
THUDD
We can do this.
SKID
!
moosh!
FLASH

THUD
THUD
SORRY.
THUD
BWOOSH

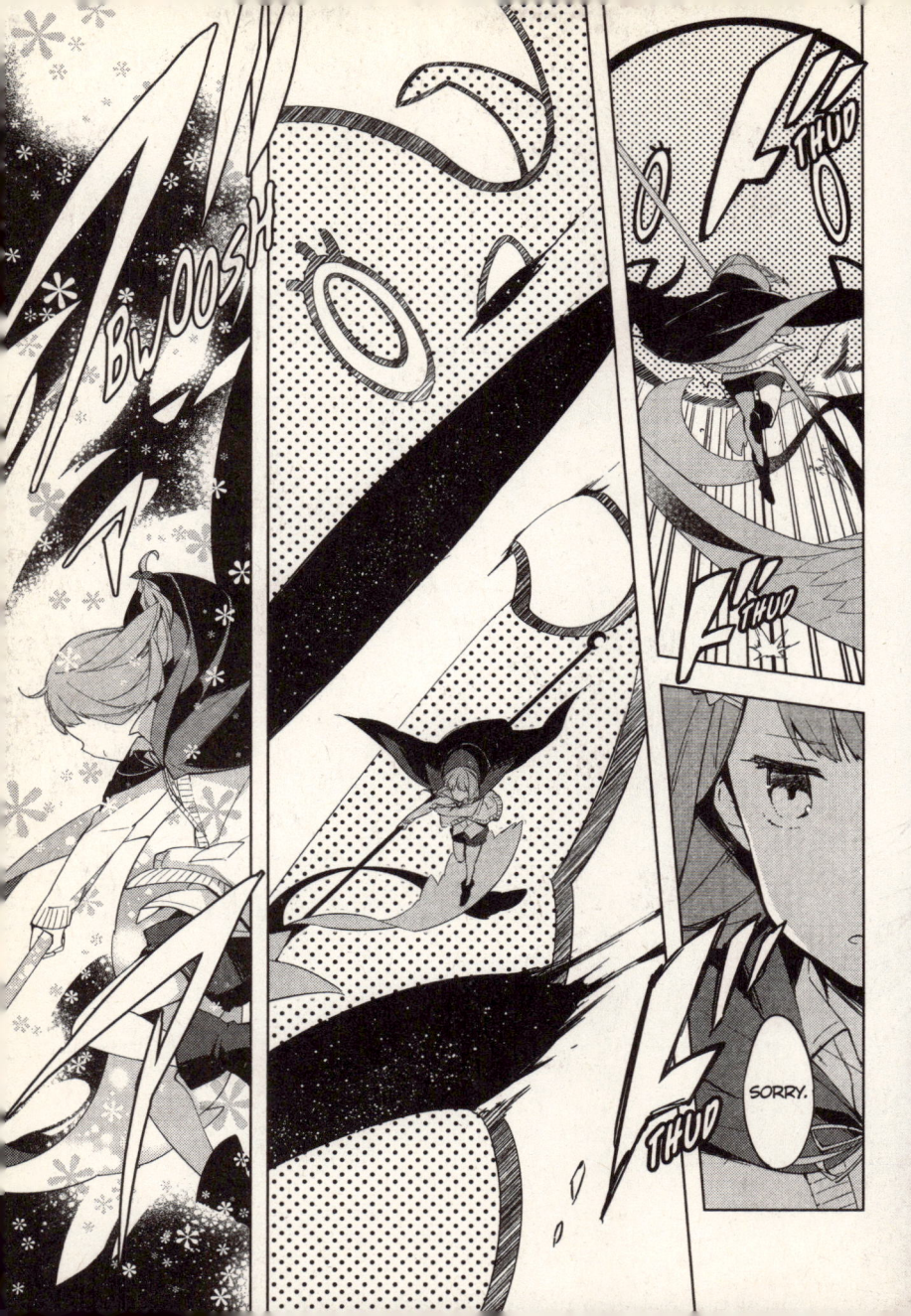

SSHAAH
JOLT
Oh!
UH... UMM...
ARE YOU... ALL RIGHT?
GRAB
ARE YOU HURT OR...
BEAM
YOU'RE AMAAAZ-ING!!
YOU CAN DEFEAT COSMOFS?!
??!

UH... UMM...?!
Oh...!
Wooow!
AH...
RUMBLE...
I'M GLAD I BROUGHT A WAGON.
RUMBLE
I'M SORRY. YOU WERE BUSY, WEREN'T YOU?
RUMBLE
RUMBLE
DON'T WORRY ABOUT ME.
MY HOUSE IS JUST OVER THERE, SO I CAN GIVE YOU FIRST AID.
WE COULD BUMP INTO ANOTHER COSMOF, THOUGH, AND...
RUMBLE...
......
THAT'S RIGHT! INTRODUCTIONS!
Nice to meet you.
I'M MIRA.
MY PARTY WAS TRAVELING BETWEEN TERRITORIES WHEN I GOT SEPARATED FROM EVERYONE.

SO, YOU'RE MIRA... NICE TO MEET YOU, TOO.
IS SHE A FOR-EIGN-ER?
I'M...
YOU'RE AMAKAWA ALICE-CHAN, AREN'T YOU...?
YOU KNEW...?
I HOPE THAT DIDN'T MAKE YOU FEEL WEIRD.
I MEAN, THE NAME "AMAKAWA," IT'S...YOU KNOW, YOU'RE FAMOUS!
FA-MOUS... HUNH.
I'M NOT THE FAMOUS ONE; THAT'S MY MOTHER...
IN A BAD WAY, THOUGH.
BUT, ALICE-CHAN, YOU MUST BE A REALLY NICE PERSON, RIGHT?
I MEAN, YOU JUST SAVED ME, AFTER ALL!
THANKS SO MUCH!

THIS IS THE FIRST TIME...
ANYONE'S EVER THANKED ME...
FOR ANYTHING TO DO WITH THE COSMOFS.
WOW~!
SO, THIS IS THE AMAKAWA MANSION THAT EVERYONE TALKS ABOUT...
Hmm..
Hmmm??
GLANCE
GLANCE
I-IS SOMETHING WRONG?

WELL, HOW SHOULD I PUT THIS?
IT'S LIKE, IT'S SO NORMAL THAT IT'S **WEIRD!**
What?
I'D ALWAYS IMAGINED THE AMAKAWAS' HOUSE WOULD LOOK LIKE SOME KIND OF FORTRESS!
Enter if you dare!!!
Welcome to Cosmof Castle
Amakawa
BOOOOM
F-FORTRESS...?!
Why?!
BECAUSE, FROM WHAT I'D HEARD ABOUT THE AMAKAWAS...
THEIR HOUSE WAS LIKE YOUR STEREOTYPICAL H.Q. OF AN EVIL ORGANIZATION PLOTTING TO TAKE OVER THE WORLD...SO THAT'S WHAT I IMAGINED.
TH-THAT'S JUST A HORRIBLE RUMOR, YOU KNOW.
I MEAN, I DON'T KNOW MUCH ABOUT THE RUMORS, BUT...
UNTIL SIX YEARS AGO...
THIS WAS JUST A PERFECTLY NORMAL HOME.
I SUPPOSE SOME THINGS WERE A **LITTLE** STRANGE...
BUT WE WERE AN ORDINARY FAMILY, THE KIND YOU'D FIND ANYWHERE.
YOU DON'T BELIEVE ME?
OF COURSE I DO!

THAT'S A PICTURE OF YOUR FAMILY, RIGHT?
EVERYONE'S SMILING.
YOU LOOK LIKE A REALLY WONDERFUL FAMILY.
......
MY MOTHER WAS A LITTLE ECCENTRIC, BUT SHE WAS FUN...
AND SHE WAS KIND. SHE WAS THE HEART OF THE HOUSE-HOLD.
THE COSMOFS ARE THE BAD ONES.
EVERYONE SAYS THAT MY MOTHER MADE THE COSMOFS FREAK OUT...
BUT THAT ISN'T TRUE.

SIX YEARS AGO, THE COSMOFS AND I TRIED TO HOUSE-SIT TOGETHER.
WHEN MY MOTHER DIDN'T RETURN...
THE COSMOFS RAN OUT TO SEARCH FOR HER. THEY JUST KEPT RUNNING AWAY.
A FEW DAYS LATER...
CRA
SSHH
News-flash! This is a news-flash!
Unknown creatures are destroying buildings!
THAT'S WHEN I FOUND OUT THAT MY MOM'S PETS...
WERE DOING SUCH UNBELIEVABLE, FRIGHTENING THINGS.
I WAS SCARED, SO I HID FROM ANY NEWS FROM THE OUTSIDE WORLD...I COULDN'T DO ANYTHING.
I KNOW... THE COSMOFS AREN'T REALLY THE BAD GUYS.
THE ONE WHO'S **REALLY** AT FAULT...
THE ONE WHO WAS SUPPOSED TO STOP THEM BACK THEN WAS...

THANKS FOR OPENING UP TO ME.

ALICE-CHAN...

THAT'S WHY I THINK I CAN HELP YOU.

YOU FEEL CONFLICTED ABOUT THE COSMOFS TOO, DON'T YOU, ALICE-CHAN?

MIRA-SAN...

I'VE BEEN THINKING ABOUT THIS FROM THE MOMENT YOU DEFEATED THAT COSMOF, ALICE-CHAN.

I THINK THAT WE'RE GOING TO BE GREAT FRIENDS.

LET'S EXTERMINATE THE COSMOFS TOGETHER, SHALL WE?

HEY, ALICE-CHAN...

......
WARNING!
INTRUDER ALERT!
!
AH!
UMM...
I'M SORRY, JUST A MOMENT!
WHAT DID SHE SAY WE'D DO TO THE COSMOFS JUST NOW...?
"EXTERMI-NATE"?
YOU ARE AMAKAWA ALICE-DONO, CORRECT?
IT LOOKS LIKE I DON'T HAVE TO BOTHER ISSUING A SUMMONS.

"THESE PEOPLE... WHO ARE THEY...?"

"AND WHO MIGHT YOU BE?! DO YOU HAVE SOME BUSINESS WITH ME?!"

"OH DEAR."

"WHAT HORRIBLE TIMING."

"JUST WHEN THINGS WERE GOING GOOD WITH ALICE! WHY ARE YOU GETTING IN MY WAY, SPICA?!"

CLACK CLACK

"MIRA...? WHAT- EEEVER. WE'LL TALK ABOUT THIS LATER."

"LET'S GET RIGHT TO THE POINT."

"PLEASE COME ALONG WITH US."

WHAT DO YOU MEAN...?
OH, I'M SORRY, *OKAAAY?* I MAY NOT HAVE TOLD YOU EVERYTHING.
YOU SEE, WE ARE HERE TO **RID THE WORLD OF THE COSMOF SCOURGE!**
TA—DA!
WE'RE HEROES FOR JUSTICE!
I HEARD THE RUMORS ABOUT HOW YOU KILL COSMOFS, ALICE-CHAN.
SO I'M HERE TO DISCUSS HOW YOU CAN HELP US!
HOW ABOUT IT, THEN?
LET'S PICK UP WHERE WE LEFT OFF. WILL YOU HELP US KILL COSMOFS?
AFTER ALL, ALICE-CHAN...
YOU DON'T WANT YOU AND YOUR FAMILY TO BE TREATED LIKE PARIAHS ANYMORE, RIGHT?
ALICE-CHAN, YOUR POWERS ARE REAL, SO WHY DON'T YOU QUIT GUARDING THIS BACKWATER TOWN AND--
I'M SORRY.

WHAT ...?!
I'M SORRY, BUT I CAN'T HELP YOU.
B-BUT WHY, ALICE-CHAN?!
I PROMISED MY MOTHER.
I'M SUPPOSED TO HOUSE-SIT UNTIL EVERYONE COMES BACK HOME... THAT'S WHAT I PROMISED.
THE COSMOFS ARE STUPID. SO...
IF I WEREN'T WATCHING THEM, THEY'D PROBABLY DESTROY THE HOUSE.
I DON'T WANT THEM TO DO THAT, AND EVEN THOUGH THE COSMOFS ARE RUNNING AMOK RIGHT NOW...
I THINK THEY'LL GO BACK TO NORMAL AS SOON AS MY MOTHER AND IMORI COME BACK, SO...
FWOOOOO
Humph!
....
HMM... I SEE.
THAT'S RIGHT--HMM. ALICE-CHAN LOVES HER HOUSE, HUH?
THEN I GUESS WE'VE GOT NO CHOICE.

DO IT.
KA
BLAM

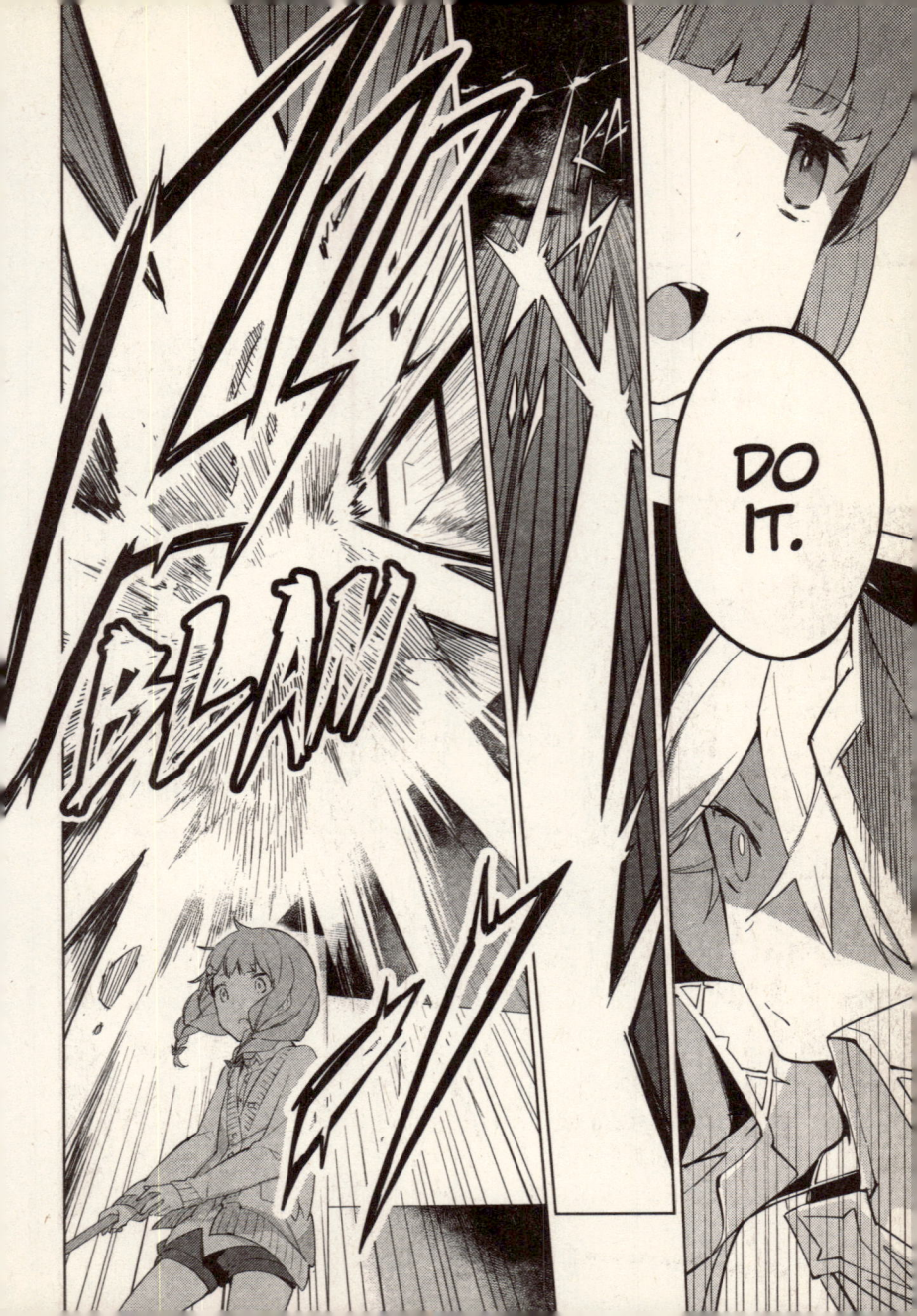

Okaay!!
ALICE-CHAN WAS A BAD GIRL, SO THE FOYER IS GONE!
CRASH
DID YOU REALLY THINK YOU COULD SAY NO, WITH THE WAY THINGS ARE?!
YOU **STILL** DON'T GET IT! YOU MISERABLE SHUT-IN!
THOSE INFERNAL PESTS ARE CAUSING WORLD-WIDE DEVASTATION!
ALL BECAUSE YOU PEOPLE **CAN'T CONTROL YOUR PETS!**
YOU WILL WITNESS THEM, AND FINISH THEM OFF WITH YOUR OWN HANDS! IT'S YOUR DUTY!
WHIRL
ARREST AMAKAWA ALICE!

SEIZE
!!
......
WHAT'S GOING ON?!
ALL I DID WAS WAIT FOR EV-ERYONE TO COME HOME...
SO WHY DOES ALL THIS HAVE TO HAPPEN TO ME?!
MOTHER-SAMA AND IMORI WILL NEVER COME HOME.
THE COSMOFS, EVERY-THING...
I WISH IT WERE ALL JUST A BAD DREAM!
YEAH, IF THIS WERE ALL REALLY JUST A DREAM, THEN...
TWINKLE
IF THIS IS A BAD DREAM, THEN JUST WAKE UP, ALICE-CHAN.
...?
WHOO
HUH?
OOOOOO
WHAT ...?
OOOOO

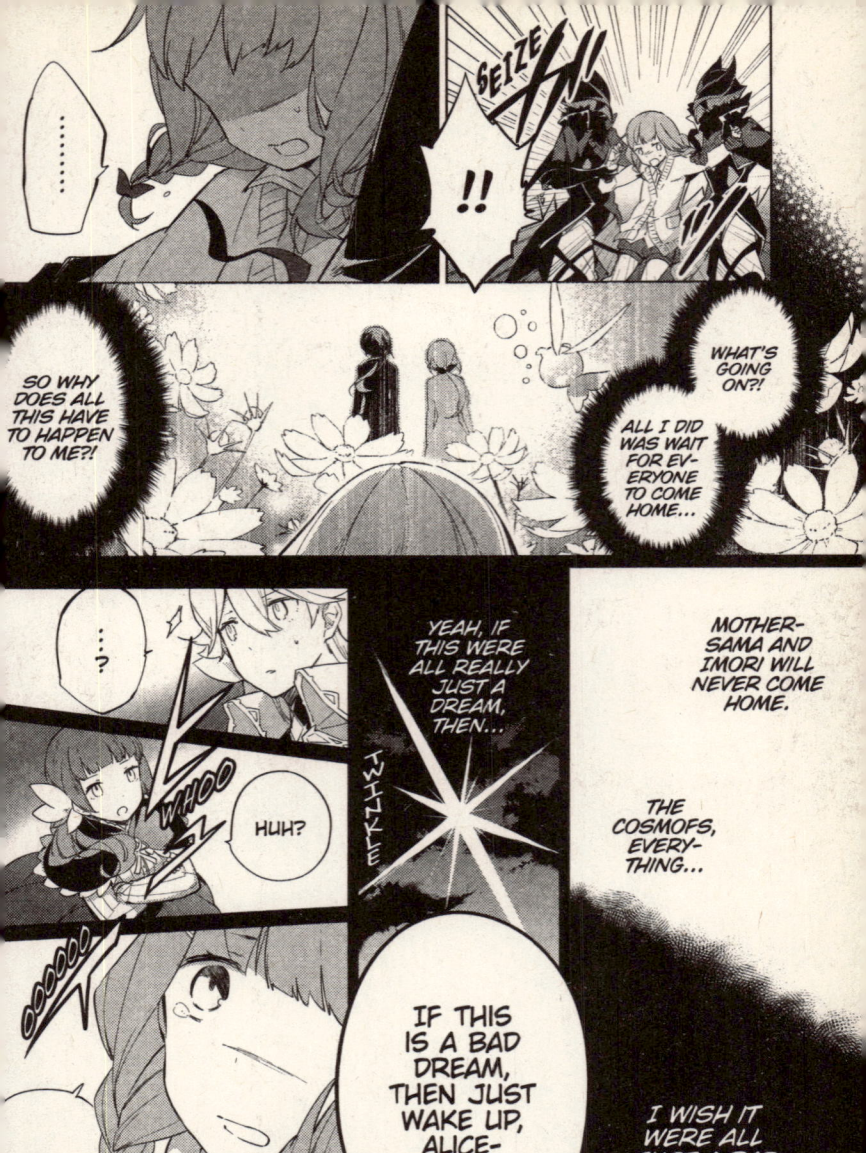

FWWW
SS
SH
HHH
FWIII
WHAT'S THIIIIIISSS ?!
A TON OF COS-MOFS?!
SSHH
WHERE ARE THEY COMING FROM ...?!
BLAM
HEY, HEY--I THINK OUR SURPRISE WAS A SUCCESS, AM I RIGHT?
WE'RE AT THE CLIMAX OF THE STORY, WHERE THE TRUE HEROES SHOW UP--IF A BIT LATE. BUT THE HOUSE IS A SHAMBLES.
WELL, WE CAN TAKE CARE OF THAT, RIGHT? NO PROBLEMS THERE!

HAPPY BIRTHDAY, ALICE!!

Huh—?!

Whaat?!

FROM MYSELF, IMORI...

AND AMAKAWA RAIKA! THIS IS...

WINK

YOUUUR BIRTHDAY PRESENT!!

Chapter 02 Cosmof

IT HAPPENED SIX YEARS AGO.

SOULFUL...

NEMIKI CITY WAS ONCE A GREEN AND PEACEFUL PLACE.

SUDDENLY, IT BECAME GROUND ZERO...

FOR A GLOBAL EPIDEMIC OF PROPERTY DAMAGE CAUSED BY VERMIN!

THERE WERE NO REPORTS OF DIRECT ATTACKS ON HUMANS OR OTHER LIVING CREATURES...
BUT ONE AFTER ANOTHER, THE VERMIN KEPT GOB-BLING UP THE ARTIFACTS OF HUMANITY.
THE CREATURES SPREAD THROUGHOUT THE WORLD IN THE BLINK OF AN EYE...
AND BEFORE LONG, THEY HAD COMPLETELY INFESTED THE LAND AND THE SKY.

JUST AS THE VERMIN KNOWN AS "COSMOFS" BEGAN THEIR INVASION...
THEIR OWNER, AMAKAWA RAIKA, DISAP-PEARED.

THE WORLD BELIEVED HER TO BE THE KEY TO THE DISASTER...

AND MANY SEARCHED FOR HER, BUT AMAKAWA RAIKA COULD NOT BE FOUND.

IS THAT HER?

IS THAT REALLY...

AMAKAWA RAIKA?

BONK
YOU'RE KIDDING, RIGHT?!
THAT'S THE AMAKAWA RAIKA?!
RAIKA-SAMA...
OKAY.
I SHALL TAKE CARE OF THIS RABBLE.
IN THAT CASE...
I'LL LEAVE THEM...
TO YOU!
BASH
WHEE!
BLOOMP
BLOOMP
?!

DID YOU JUST SAY, "AMAKAWA RAIKA"?
ARE YOU REALLY... MY MOTHER ...?
LONG TIME NO SEEE———!!!
GLOMP
AAAAH—?!
There, there, there!
LOOK HOW BIG YOU'VE GOTTEN ~!
HAVE YOU BEEN ALL RIGHT ?!
YOU DO REMEMBER ME, DON'T YOU ?????
I...
OF COURSE I REMEMBER.

SHOVE
ARE...
ARE YOU REALLY, TRULY...
MY MOTHER...?!
Yep, yep.
I BET YOU HAVE A LOT OF QUESTIONS AND THINGS TO TELL ME, HMM?
YOU...SEEM SMALLER THAN I REMEMBER, THOUGH!
SHORTY.
BUT THIS REALLY ISN'T...
THE RIGHT TIME AND PLACE FOR THIS TALK, NOW IS IT?
SO, ALICE!
Whoa?!

LET'S MAKE LIKE HERMES!!
WH-WHAAT?!
ZOOM
THEY FLEW OFF?!
A-AFTER THEM, YOU TWO!
DON'T LET ALICE ESCA--
WHOOSH
BOOF!
BONK

"QUITE THE BOISTEROUS GUEST, AREN'T YOU?"

BOOP

FWSH

"THIS FAMILY HAS BEEN REUNITED AFTER A LONG ABSENCE."

"PLEASE REFRAIN FROM RAINING ON THEIR PARADE. I, IMORI, WILL ATTEND TO YOU."

"ARGH...! HOW DARE YOU?! CRUSH THEM!"

"M-MIRA-SAMA... OUR ORDERS SAY TO AVOID ENDANGERING CIVILIANS AT ALL COSTS..."

"THAT PERSON IS A MENACE WHO IS USING VERMIN TO CAUSE CHAOS!"

"IT DOESN'T MATTER! THAT'S AN ORDER!"

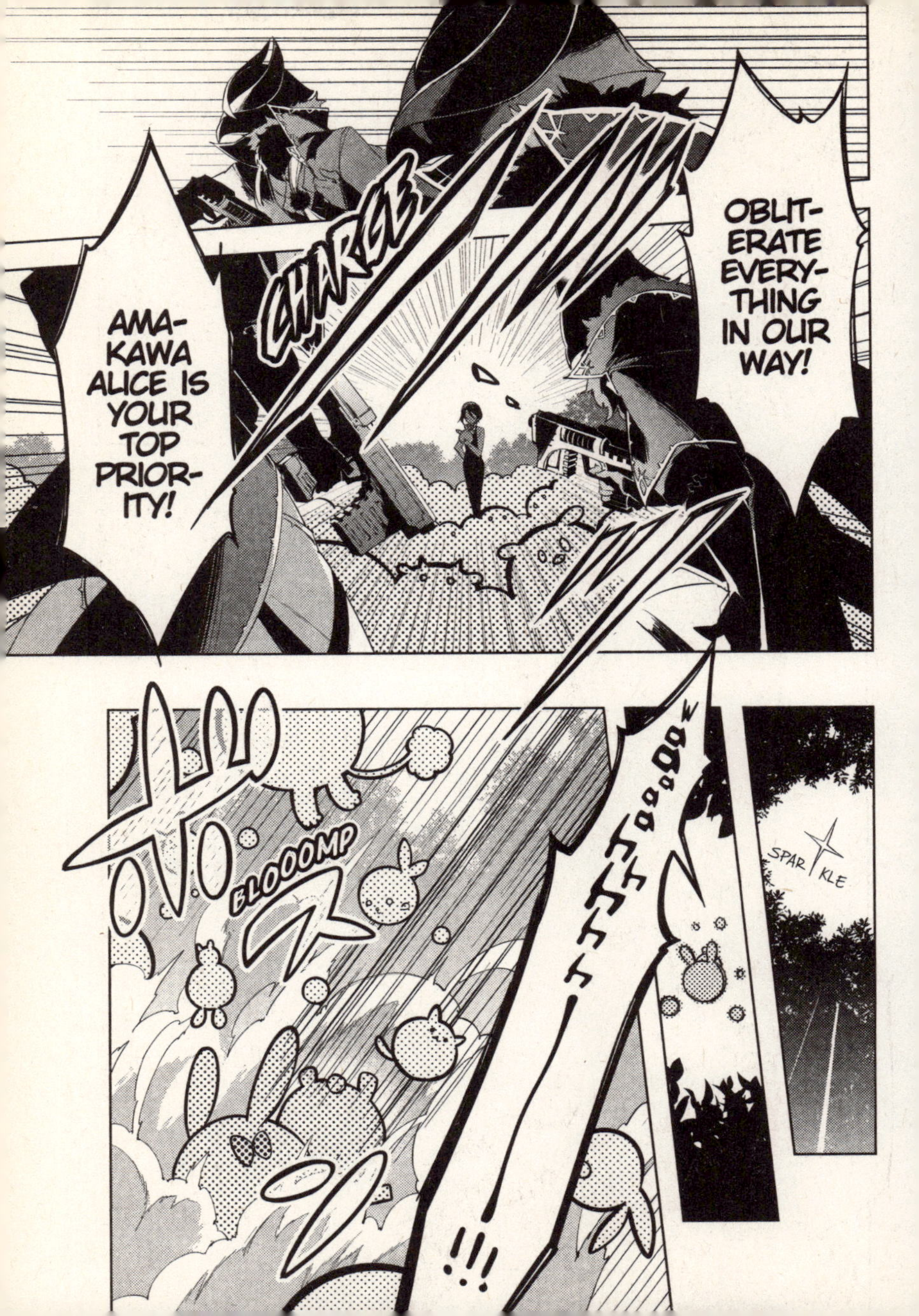
OBLIT-ERATE EVERY-THING IN OUR WAY!
CHARGE
AMA-KAWA ALICE IS YOUR TOP PRIOR-ITY!
SPAR KLE
BLOOOMP
!!!

WHSHH...

Cough! Cough!

WHAT'S REALLY GOING ON HERE...?

YEP, THAT'S RIGHT.

THIS IS...

THIS WAS MOTHER-SAMA'S FAVORITE PLACE...
ALICE AND MOTHER-SAMA'S SPECIAL SECRET HIDEAWAY.
WE CAN TALK HERE, RIGHT?
......
MOTHER-SAMA, WHEN YOU AND IMORI GOT BACK...
I WAS GOING TO BE REALLY MAD AT YOU. AT LEAST, THAT'S WHAT I THOUGHT.
I CAN... GET MAD, CAN'T I?
AFTER ALL...YOU REALLY *ARE* MOTHER-SAMA, AREN'T YOU?

YEP, YOU CAN GET MAD, ALICE.
PAT...
MOTHER-SAMA IS THE BAD ONE. MOTHER-SAMA COULDN'T ...
KEEP HER PROMISE.
PAT
PAT
PAT
PAT
PAT
NO.
I COULDN'T KEEP MY PROMISE, EITHER.
BECAUSE I COULDN'T STOP THE COSMOFS...
A LOT OF BEAUTIFUL GARDENS AND TOWNS ARE MESSED UP.
OUR HOUSE IS ALL TRASHED...
AND EVERYTHING'S GONE WRONG.

YOU KNOW, THE TOWNSPEOPLE SAY HORRIBLE THINGS ABOUT YOU, MOTHER-SAMA.

THEY SAY YOU'RE THE ONE WHO SENT THE COSMOFS ON THEIR RAMPAGE.

THEY SPREAD RUMORS...

BUT I CAN'T SAY ANYTHING TO COUNTER THEM.

NO, IT'S THE TRUTH, ALICE.

I HAVE TO TELL YOU THE TRUTH.

I'M SORRY. JUST AS WE'VE FINALLY REUNITED...

WHAT...?

THE COSMOFS RUINED THE WORLD...

AND IT REALLY IS MY FAULT. RAIKA'S FAULT.

WE, RAIKA AND IMORI, ARE COSMOFS WHO HAVE TAKEN ON THE FORMS...
OF THE ONES YOU LOVED.
THE RAIKA AND IMORI THAT YOU KNEW...
ARE NO LONGER IN THIS WORLD.
THOOM

SLAM SLAM SLAM SLAM SLAM

MIRA-SAMA, IT'S NO USE!

WHEW!

WHAT SHALL YOU DO? WILL YOU SURRENDER?

NOW THAT I AM FREE, WOULD YOU LIKE A SPOT OF TEA?

HE'S CONTROLLING THE COSMOFS!

WE'RE HELPLESS AGAINST THEM!

YOU... YOU INFERNAL PESTS!

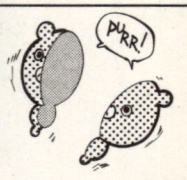

NOW, MAY I SUGGEST YOU RE-TREAT?

YOU MUST ALREADY KNOW THIS, NO?

ATTACK AS OFTEN AS YOU LIKE, BUT IT WILL BE FUTILE.

AFTER ALL, THE COSMOFS ARE IMMORTAL.

GRRRR!

Humph!

SLASH

YOU GOTTA BE KIDDING ME!

FLASH

!

OUR WEAPON, AMAKAWA ALICE, TO SEND THE COSMOFS TO THEIR GRAVES!

WE NEED...

CRACK

PURR!

POP

THAT'S WHY...

THUD
THE SATELLITE THUNDER BULLET ...
JUST MADE A DIRECT HIT TO THE TARGET.
HMM!
THIS IS BECAUSE YOU WON'T COOPER-ATE!
ROAR...
THE FACT THAT YOU TREAT OUR ALICE AS A WEAPON...
ANGERS EVEN ME.
!
WHA...!
NOW I DEFINITELY CANNOT LET YOU HAVE ALICE.
MOTHER-SAMA...
ISN'T IN THIS WORLD? WHAT DO YOU MEAN?
HEY!
GRAB
I MEAN ...

N...NO! DO YOU MEAN MOTHER-SAMA...
HAS D-DIED?!
O-okay..!
CALM DOWN!
!
IT'S ALL RIGHT! RAIKA IS ALIVE!
I PROMISE YOU!
YOU HAVE MY WORD AS A COSMOF!
THEN MY MOM AND EVERYONE ELSE ARE...
WHERE?
RIGHT NOW, ALL I CAN TELL YOU IS THAT THEY'RE ALL RIGHT.
THE REASON WHY ALL THE COSMOFS IN THE WORLD ARE RUNNING WILD...
IS BECAUSE RAIKA "DISAPPEARED" FROM THIS WORLD...
AND THE COSMOFS HAVE NO LEADER.

WE ARE SEARCHING FOR OUR OWNER, RAIKA...
AND WE ALSO HAVE TO STOP THE RAMPAGING COSMOFS.
ALICE...
THE REASON WE HAVE COME TO YOU...
IS THAT WE HAVE SOMETHING VERY IMPORTANT TO ASK.
I WILL TAKE YOU TO WHERE RAIKA IS, ALICE.
WOULD YOU PLEASE BRING OUR RAIKA BACK?

STOP RIGHT THERE!
RUSTLE
AMAKAWA ALICE, COME HERE.
YOU'RE THE ONE...
WHO DESTROY-ED MY HOUSE!
DUN
DUN
DUN!
I AM CALLED SPICA...
BUT THAT IS NOT IMPOR-TANT!
This can't be good!
ALICE, ARE YOU REALLY GOING TO BELIEVE THEM?
THEY SAY THEY CAN REUNITE YOU WITH PEOPLE WHO HAVE BEEN MISS-ING FOR SIX YEARS.
DON'T YOU THINK THAT'S TOO GOOD TO BE TRUE?
I REGRET THE EXCESSIVE FORCE WE USED TO TRY TO PERSUADE YOU EARLIER...
AND, OF COURSE, WE WILL REPAIR YOUR HOUSE.
WE JUST WANT YOUR HELP TO EXTERMINATE THE COSMOFS FOR THE BENEFIT OF THE WORLD.

I ALSO HEAR THAT YOU ARE SLANDERED BY THE TOWNSPEOPLE, CORRECT?
......
WE, HOWEVER, WOULD WELCOME YOU WITH OPEN ARMS.
IF YOU COME WITH US, WE CAN PROMISE YOU CLOTHING, FOOD, SHELTER, AND PROTECTION... WHAT DO YOU SAY?
GRASP
SLIDE...
I'VE KNOWN FOR A WHILE NOW...
THE COSMOFS ARE FAMILY...
BUT I HAVE TO DO SOMETHING ABOUT THEM.
THEN--
BUT!
YANK
I... DON'T WANT TO HURT THE COSMOFS ANYMORE, SO...
SPRING
I'M GOING TO GET MOTHER-SAMA AND IMORI BACK!

WH- WHY?!
FIRST OF ALL, I DON'T TRUST SKETCHY PEOPLE WHO DRESS WEIRD AND DESTROY MY FOYER!!
......!!!!
ALICE ...
I REALLY DON'T KNOW WHAT TO BELIEVE!
IF I GO WITH YOU, I'M REALLY GOING TO SEE THEM, RIGHT?!
PLEASE! TAKE ME!
OF COURSE I WILL!
PLEASE COME WITH ME TO THE BUSHES OVER THERE.
WE'RE WALKING?

I TOTALLY THOUGHT WE WERE GOING TO WARP OUT OR SOMETHING.

Like when you appeared.

It's this way. This way.

RUSTLE
RUSTLE

HEY... IS MOTHER-SAMA REALLY DOWN THIS WAY?

HERE IT IS.

RUSTLE

I'M SORRY, I DON'T UNDERSTAND WHAT YOU'RE SAYING.

THE WAY TO RAIKA IS THROUGH THIS OLD WELL.

Danger!! Old Well

HUH...?

No way. Totally impossible!!!!
It's all right!!
It's all right, you'll see!!!!
RUSTLE
I FOUND THEM, BUT...
RUSTLE
THOSE KIDS... WHAT ARE THEY DOING OVER THERE?
No, I'll die!
You're gonna kill me!
Go!!!!!
...?!
CRUNCH
RUSH
CRUNCH
W-WAIT... WAIT!!
I DON'T UNDERSTAND... YOU'VE STILL GOT SO MUCH TO LIVE FOR!
TRIP
Huh??!
WHU?

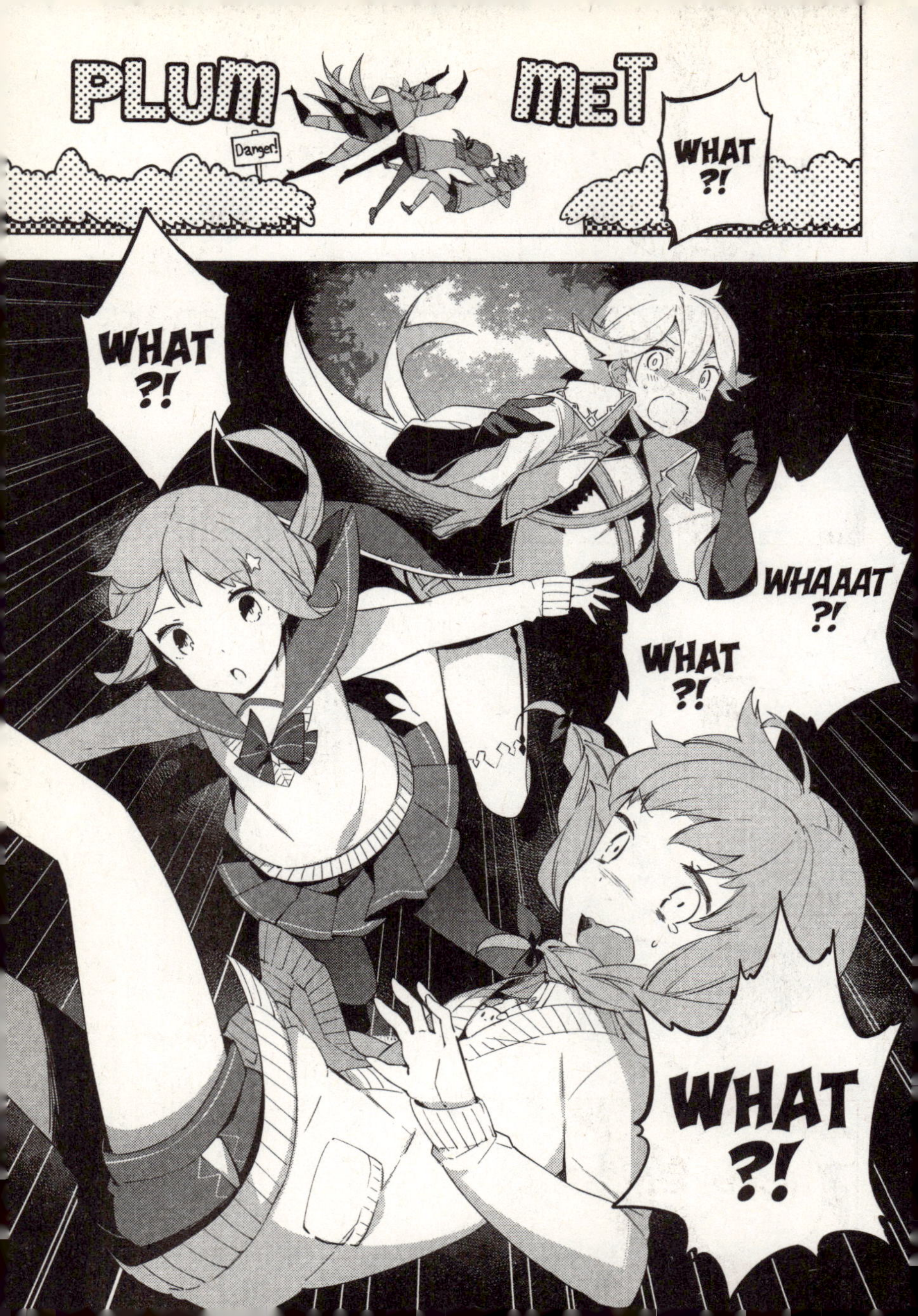
PLUM MET
Danger!
WHAT ?!
WHAAAT ?!
WHAT ?!
WHAT ?!
WHAT ?!

SO, THEY'VE DEPARTED SAFELY.

I SEE.

......

MY WORK HERE IS DONE!

I SURRENDER!

CLAP
CLAP

THUS HAVE I PLAYED MY PART.

OHHH, EXCUSE ME!

OH NO, MIRA-CHAN!

WHAT ARE YOU UP TO?!

S-SURRENDER?!

IT LOOKS LIKE WE'VE KIND OF, WELL... STOPPED RECEIVING SPICA'S LIFE SIGNS?
?
SPICA'S... WHAT?!
YOU! WHAT DID YOU DO WITH SPICA?!
WHO KNOWS...? I DO NOT THINK SPICA IS DEAD.
PERHAPS SHE WAS SPIRITED AWAY ALONG WITH ALICE?
SPRIN
KLE
WELL... YOU MIGHT MEET THEM IF YOU ARE LUCKY.
RO
NGH?!
WAIT...! DON'T RUN AWAY!!
OOAA
SPICA?... NO... WHERE DID YOU TAKE ALICE?
WHO ON EARTH ARE YOU?!
AARR

THE ANSWER TO YOUR FIRST QUESTION IS A SECRET. HOWEVER, I SHALL ANSWER YOUR SECOND.

WE ARE THE ONES YOU KNOW VERY WELL, THE ONES YOU DESPISE.

WE ARE THE CUTE ALIENS.

WE ARE THE COSMOFS.

Chapter 03 Alice
SHHHH
ALL THE COSMOFS AROUND US...
HAVE DISAPPEARED, IT SEEMS...
WITHOUT A TRACE.
SSHH
WHAT IN THE WORLD IS GOING ON...?
....

BEEP BEEP

"THIS IS MIRA."

"WHAT ARE THEY, ANYWAY? I'VE NEVER HEARD OF HUMANOID COSMOFS..."

"We reviewed the data you sent earlier."

WHIRRR

"YES. WE FAILED."

"The unidentified Cosmofs are currently under investigation."

"Your hard work is appreciated. Please return immediately."

"WAIT! I NEED TO GO AFTER SPICA!"

"IF I COULD GET PERMISSION FOR "TRANSFORM," THEN THEY WOULDN'T BE..."

!

"There is no need for that."

I HAVE AN IDEA CONCERNING SPICA'S WHEREABOUTS.

OUR GOAL WAS MERELY TO MAKE CONTACT WITH AMAKAWA ALICE.

ALL PERSONNEL ARE TO RETURN AND REGROUP.

Is that understood?

YOU WON'T ESCAPE ME!

HUMPH.

CLICK

UNDERSTOOD.

BONK

?!

HUH? I...

WHAT WAS I DOING?

MY BODY FEELS HEAVY.

EVERYTHING IS TINGLING...

WHO IS...?

I'M SORRY I DRAGGED YOU IN HERE LIKE THAT.

I'M THE COSMOF FROM EARLIER.

I'M RAIKA'S PET AND... A MEMBER OF YOUR FAMILY.

......

I KNOW ABOUT YOUR CHILDHOOD... AND, OF COURSE, ABOUT RAIKA, TOO.	BUT I KNOW YOU.

WHO ON EARTH ARE YOU?

I...I'VE NEVER SEEN ANYONE LIKE YOU.

ALICE, THE MOTHER-SAMA YOU KNOW...

IS SOMEWHERE UP AHEAD. I PROMISE.

I KNOW YOU'LL BE ABLE TO FIND HER, ALICE.

SNAP

PLEASE BRING BACK... OUR RAIKA.

ROAR
I MUST BID YOU FARE-WELL HERE.
AHH!
I HOPE WE'LL MEET AGAIN... SOONER RATHER THAN LATER.
HEY!
DON'T LEAVE ME HERE!
I DON'T UNDER-STAND ANY-THING YET!
WAAAAAAAI—

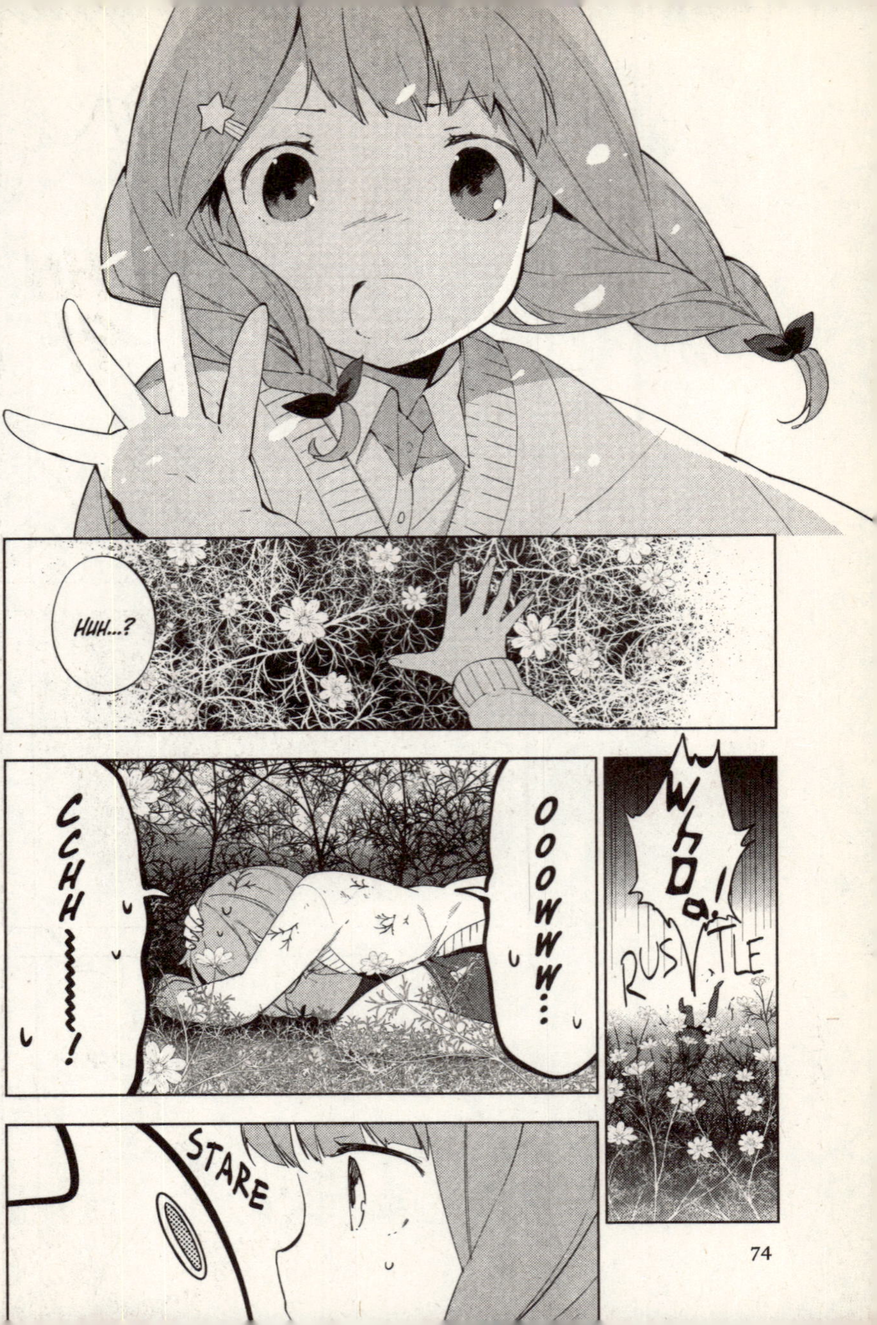
HUH...?
WHOA!!
RUSTLE
OOOWWW...
CCHH~~~!
STARE

RUSTLE
WAG WAG
C....COSMOF?!

AHH?!

BO BOLD

*WHERE AM I...?

CREAK...
YOU CAN'T JUST RUN OFF ON YOUR OWN LIKE THAT...
WHAT'S WRONG WITH YOU? REALLY!

PAPII~!
Boing!

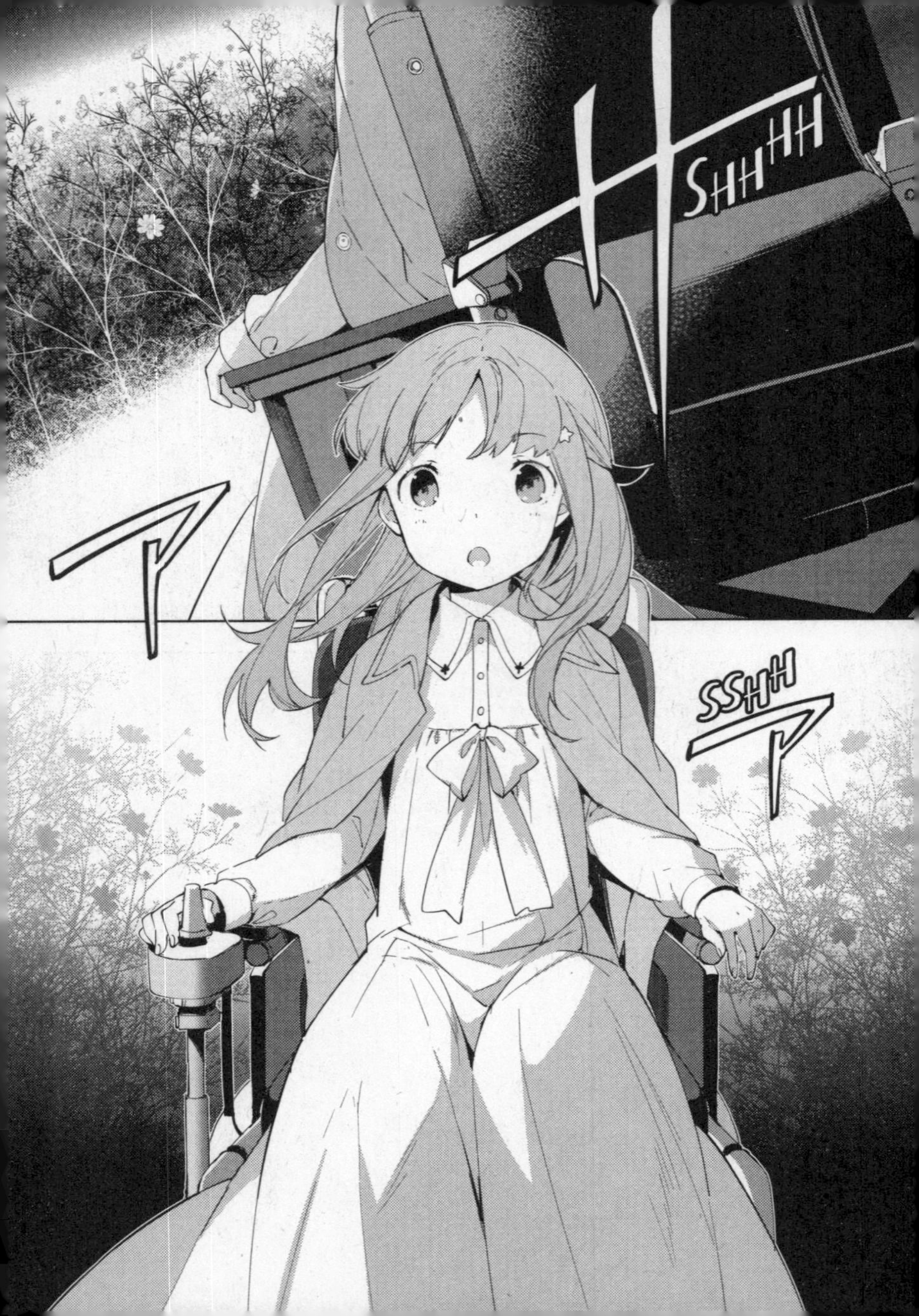
SHHHH
SSHHH

SSHH
I TOLD YOU NOT TO...
SSHH

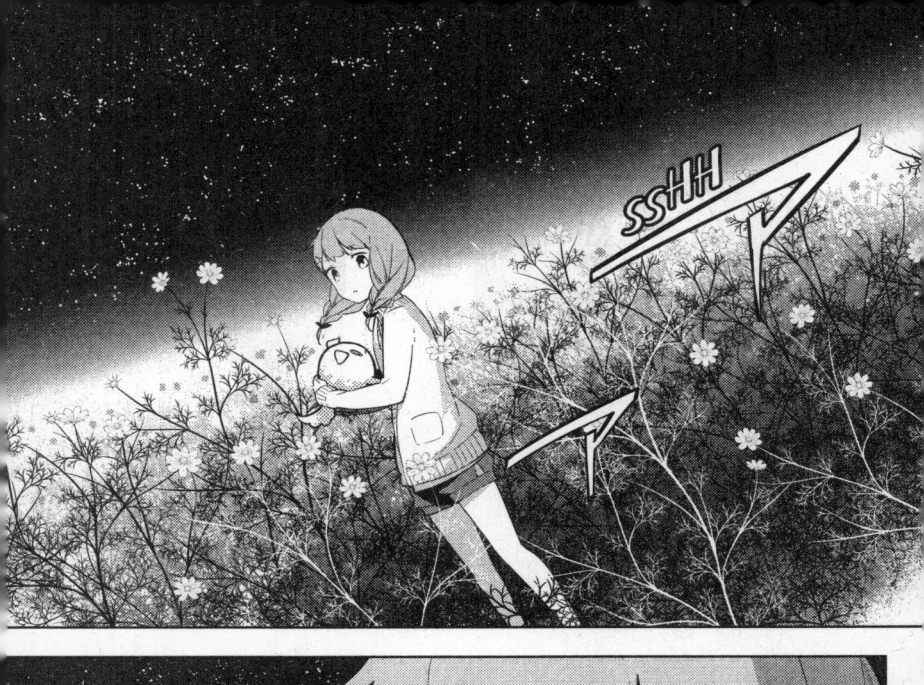

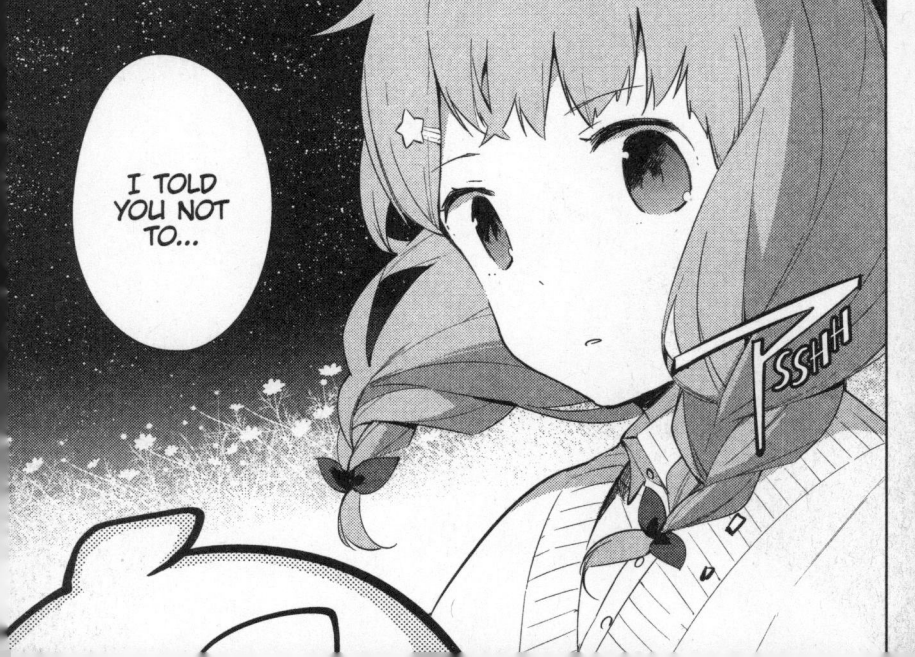

Boing!
......
SHE LOOKS EXACTLY LIKE ME.
WHAT?
GRAB
?!
WHUMP
Not good
TAP
TAP
Excuse me?
Someone who looks exactly like me is he
Outside!!!
TAP
TAP
UH...
UMM?
ZSH
ZSH
ZSH

SLIDE
RAIKA-SAMAAAAAA!
WHAT IS THE MAAAAT-TERRRR?!
SKID
WHAAAH——?!
WHAT SCOUN-DREL SEEKS TO DECEIVE US BY USING RAIKA-SAMA'S LIKE-NESS?
WHAT SORT OF...
TH...
THIS IS...!

YOU ARE QUITE CORRECT.

SEE? LOOK! THE SAME FACE!

......

WHAT IS THE MEANING OF THIS?

I DON'T UNDERSTAND EITHER, IMORI!

"RAIKA" AND...

"IMORI"?

IS THIS ONE OF THOSE... YOU KNOW, WHERE IF YOU SEE IT YOU DIE...?

YOU MEAN A DOPPELGÄNGER? THAT'S HIGHLY UNLIKELY.

ARE THESE TWO IMPOSTORS, TOO?!

UM, AHH!

AND YOU ARE...?

EXCUSE ME, BUT WHO MIGHT YOU BE?
YOU ARE ON AMAKAWA PROPERTY...
BUT WHAT'S YOUR BUSINESS WITH US AT SUCH A LATE HOUR?
WHAT ...?
THEY DON'T KNOW ME...
AND WORSE YET, THEY'RE SUSPICIOUS OF ME!
GLARE...
I-I'M SORRY! UM, UHH...!
ALICE.
MY NAME IS ALICE.
I CAME HERE LOOKING FOR MY MO-- SOMEONE, AND...
WELL, I'M HERE, BUT...

"WHILE I WAS LOOKING FOR SOMEONE...

I FELL INTO A WEIRD OLD WELL... AND THAT'S ALL I CAN REMEMBER."

"SORRY. I DON'T REALLY UNDERSTAND MY SITUATION, EITHER.

WHEN I CAME TO, I WAS HERE, AND I DON'T REALLY KNOW WHAT'S GOING ON."

"OLD WELL"?

"CAN WE TAKE HER HOME WITH US?!"

BEAM

"HEY... IMORI..."

"YES...?"

? ?

RAIKA-SAMA... IMPULSIVELY BRINGING HOME A STRANGER LIKE THIS IS...

PLEASE!

I... understand.

MY APOLOGIES, ALICE-SAN.

WITH REGARD TO YOUR SEARCH...

HAVE YOU IDENTIFIED ANY LIKELY PLACES TO INVESTIGATE?

NO. NOT AT ALL.

THEN...

PLEASE JOIN US AT OUR RESIDENCE.

WELCOME TO AMAKAWA HOUSE.

WE DO NOT HAVE MUCH, BUT WE'RE HAPPY TO SHARE.

"AMA-KAWA HOUSE"...

TICK...
TOCK...

TICK...
TOCK...

TICK...

PAPII ISN'T GIVING ME A WARNING...

STARE....

NO MATTER HOW I LOOK AT IT, IT LOOKS JUST LIKE MY HOUSE.

ROLL ROLL

"ALICE, THE MOTHER-SAMA YOU KNOW..."

"IS SOMEWHERE UP AHEAD. I PROMISE."

And now for the local news.

THEN WHO... ARE THESE TWO?

Negoki City's own Ougi Academy, a private girls' high school...
opened its school festival today.
HARVEST FESTIV
The school was founded two years ago...
and, with the local residents...
WHAT?
OH!
WE SHOULD PROBABLY INTRODUCE OURSELVES, HUH?
I AM RAIKA!
AMAKAWA RAIKA!
AND THIS IS...
I AM IMORI, THE LIVE-IN HELP.

I HOPE OUR ABRUPT INVITATION DID NOT STARTLE YOU.

AND THIS IS MY PET, PAPII!

PAPII...

THIS IS A REMOTE AREA, SO WE DO NOT RECEIVE MANY VISITORS.

WOULD YOU MIND ACCOMPANYING RAIKA-SAMA FOR A WHILE?

I...I SEE.

NOW EVERYTHING IS READY.

SMILE

ABOUT THAT "OLD WELL" YOU MENTIONED EARLIER...

I THINK WE MAY BE ABLE TO HELP YOU WITH THAT.

!

IN HONOR OF ALICE, WHO BROUGHT ABOUT THIS EXTRAORDI-NARY MEETING...
I HAVE PREPARED A HIGH TEA TO CELEBRATE THIS "UN-HOLIDAY."
HOW NAUGHTY OF YOU TO SET UP A TEA PARTY THIS LATE AT NIGHT!
PLEASE DO NOT SPEAK OF THIS TO YOUR FATHER.
UMM... IT'S SO FANCY.
ARE YOU SURE IT'S ALL RIGHT IF I HAVE SOME?
WHAT? YES!
BUT OF COURSE!
PLEASE HAVE AS MUCH AS YOU LIKE.

IS THE FARE NOT TO YOUR LIKING?

CLINK...

NO... THAT'S NOT IT.

JUST THE OP-POSITE.
THIS...
IS WHAT I HAVE WANTED FOR SO LONG!
EVEN ON MY BIRTHDAY, ALL I HAD WAS A SINGLE DRY BISCUIT.
I DREAM ABOUT EATING STUFF LIKE THIS ALL THE TIME!
EVEN IF I DON'T REALLY KNOW...
WHERE I AM...
AND IF THE PEOPLE IN FRONT OF ME ARE "REAL" OR NOT.

AT LEAST I KNOW THESE FLAVORS AND SCENTS...
ARE REAL.
IT'S FUNNY HOW AN "UN-HOLIDAY" CAN BE FANCIER THAN A BIRTHDAY, ISN'T IT?
THE TEA AND THE TREATS ARE TRULY DELICIOUS.
THANK YOU.
I'M HAPPY TO MAKE YOU HAPPY.
SAY, MAY I... CALL YOU JUST "ALICE"?
S-SURE. I DON'T MIND, BUT...
UMM, SO... ALICE...

Panel	
WELL, I'VE BEEN WAITING.	DO YOU... HAVE TO GO BACK TO YOUR SEARCH RIGHT AWAY?
WAITING FOR SOMEONE LIKE YOU TO COME ALONG.	WHAT?

I WANT TO TALK WITH YOU...

A WHOLE, WHOLE LOT MORE.

BUT...

IF YOU DON'T MIND...

I... WANT TO BE YOUR FRIEND, ALICE!

HU

WHOoOOSHH

SQUELCH

NNGH...

TRANSMIS-
SIONS...
DOWN.

SILENCE...

LOCATION
INFORMATION UN-
AVAILABLE.

RUSTLE

IT'S
NO
USE...

MIRA...
COM-
MANDING
OFFICER...

AKANE-
CHAN...

SHIZUKI-
CHAN...

SNIFFLE...

I'VE LOST... EVERYONE!!

Waaaah—

EVERYBODYYYY!!!

WHERE... AM I...?!

Chapter 09 Raika

CHEEP...
CHEEP CHEEP

Mmm...

SO WARM...

SMELLS LIKE SUNSHINE...

SMELLS LIKE BREAKFAST.

OOH, THIS MUST BE...

HEAVEN, RIGHT...?

SO BOLD.

LURCH

Woah!

CHEEP CHEEP...

......

PLOP

WAG WAG

DÉJÀ VU...!

LAP LAP

HOW WAS BREAKFAST?

YOU'VE ALREADY LENT ME A ROOM AND A CHANGE OF CLOTHES...

BUT BREAKFAST, TOO? THAT'S SO...

PLEASE DO NOT WORRY ABOUT IT.

YOU ARE THE ONE WHO IS INDULGING RAIKA, AFTER ALL.

IT WAS DELICIOUS.

THANK YOU VERY MUCH.

FROM THAT MOMENT, I...

MAY I SHOW ALICE THE GARDEN TODAY?

AS YOU WISH, BUT DO NOT TAX YOURSELF TOO MUCH.

"I... want to be your friend, Alice!"

IT WILL AFFECT YOUR HEALTH, YOU KNOW.

I knoooow.

BECAME RAIKA'S FRIEND...

AND HER CONVERSATION PARTNER.

SHE TALKED ABOUT WHAT SHE SAW AROUND HER.

I'm always home, so all I know is anime, manga, and my smartphone. The only other thing I do is play with Papi!!

I've also gotten into urban legends lately and... Does this make sense to you? Do you understand what I'm saying??

Sure, sure.

Pretty much.

I JUST NODDED, BUT...

SHE TALKED ABOUT WHAT HAPPENED TO HER EACH DAY.

FROM WHAT RAIKA SAID...

AND THEN, YOU KNOW, OUGI ACADEMY IS DOWN AT THE BOTTOM OF THE HILL.

AND THE INFORMATION I HAVE PICKED UP...

THEY BUILT THE SCHOOL LAST YEAR BUT...

"Records say it was...Ougi Academy a private high school for girls"

I CAN'T REALLY BELIEVE THIS, BUT I SEEM TO BE...

"Wasn't it a school before it got trashed?"

I'M PRETTY SURE.

THUD

WHAT WAS THAT NOISE FROM THE FOYER?

I SHALL GO CHECK.

HMM?

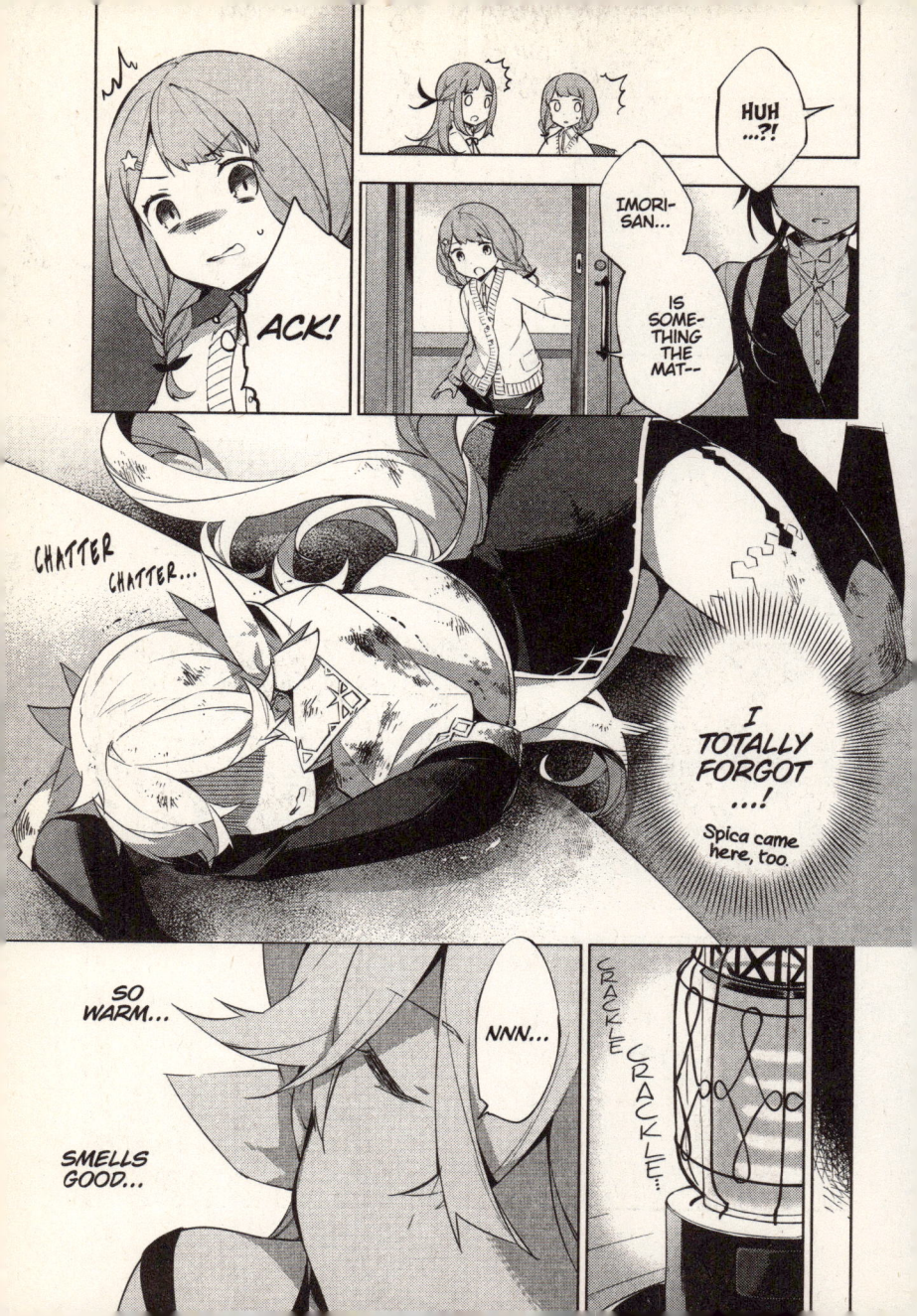

HUH ...?!
IMORI-SAN...
IS SOMETHING THE MAT--
ACK!
I TOTALLY FORGOT ...!
Spica came here, too.
CHATTER CHATTER...
CRACKLE CRACKLE...
NNN...
SO WARM...
SMELLS GOOD...

HEA... VEN...?

THIS MUST BE...

RUSTLE

THANK GOODNESS.

IT SEEMS SHE IS AWAKE, ALICE-SAN.

?!
....
?!!

Excuse me...?

Ummm...

I hear you are an acquaintance of Alice-san?

Well, then... It is time for Raika-sama to take her medicine, so please excuse us.

Yes, I'm so sorry for all this trouble.

Though it is only the beginning of autumn, it is cold outside.

Please rest until you are fully warmed.

....

KER-CLUNK...

Wh... what is going on here...?!

I told them that I knew you.

I DIDN'T WANT THEM TO GET SUS-PICIOUS AND MAKE A BIG FUSS.
AND WHO ARE THOSE TWO I JUST TALKED TO--
DON'T YOU LAY A FINGER ON THEM!
THEY HAVE NOTHING TO DO WITH ANY-THING!
JUMP
WHAT?!
DO YOU KNOW SOME-THING ABOUT THIS PLACE?!
TWENTY YEARS.
I THINK I HAVE A PRETTY GOOD IDEA.
THIS IS MY HOUSE... FROM TWENTY YEARS AGO.

THE TWO PEOPLE YOU MET EARLIER ARE...

MY FAMILY, FROM BACK THEN.

TWENTY YEARS AGO! YOU MUST BE KID--

IF YOU DON'T BELIEVE ME...

GO LOOK AT THE NEWS-PAPERS, TV, OR ANYTHING ELSE.

"EMPEROR... ASCENDS TO THE THRONE... NEW YEAR'S EDITION..." ...?

THIS ALL HAPPENED BEFORE I WAS BORN...

THE TWO PEOPLE HERE AREN'T THE SAME ONES AS YOUR ENEMIES... UNDERSTAND?

......

I TOLD THEM I WAS LOOKING FOR SOMEONE, BUT I DIDN'T TELL THEM WHO I WAS.
AFTER YOU'VE WARMED UP, JUST LEAVE...
AND DON'T BOTHER US ANYM--
W-WAIT A MINUTE!
CRUSH
IF THAT'S TRUE, THEN HOW DO I GET BACK TO MY PEOPLE?!
HUH?
THUMP
NO WONDER MY COMMUNICATIONS DEVICE DOESN'T WORK!
WHAT...? I DON'T KNOW!
YOU'LL HAVE TO FIGURE THAT OUT YOURSELF!
NO WONDER I COULDN'T FIND THEM, THOUGH I WALKED ALL NIGHT...
OUTSIDE...IT WAS SO COLD...

?!

SNIFF...

HOW DID THIS HAPPEN...?

OH NO... DON'T CRY!

IT'S JUST HAPPENED TO ME TOO, AND I DON'T KNOW HOW TO GET BACK, EITHER!

UMM, SO, WHO **ARE** YOU GUYS, ANYWAY?

YOU'RE NOT EXACTLY ORDINARY FOLKS, ARE YOU?

I...I'M NOT CRYING... THIS IS... SWEAT.

WHIP

Y-YOU'RE RIGHT! I OWE YOU A PROPER INTRODUCTION!

SHE DOESN'T SEEM QUITE LIKE THE SAME PERSON.

They have business cards...!
EXCUSE ME FOR NOT INTRODUCING MYSELF FORMALLY THE OTHER DAY.
I AM OFFICIALLY KNOWN AS SPICA.
I BELONG TO AN ORGANIZATION CALLED **NIX.**
NIX?
YES. OUR JOB IS TO APPREHEND BEINGS THAT DID NOT ORIGINATE ON THIS PLANET.
IN RECENT YEARS OUR ACTIVITIES FOCUSED ON THE LOWLY COSMOFS.
TO PUT IT SIMPLY, YOU MIGHT SAY WE ARE POLICE WHO TARGET THE COSMOFS.
COSMOFS...
FROM WHAT OCCURRED EARLIER, IT IS ONLY NATURAL...
THAT YOU MIGHT THINK WE ARE UNSCRUPULOUS AND DISTRUST US.

HOWEVER, FOR THE TIME BEING...
CAN'T WE COOPER-ATE?
YOU'RE SEARCHING FOR SOME-ONE, AND I NEED TO GET HOME. WE CAN HELP EACH OTHER.
......
CLUTCH...
I TOLD YOU BEFORE-- I'M NOT JOINING FORCES WITH YOU.
BUT YOU **DO** HAVE A POINT.
AT LEAST FOR NOW, EXCHANGING INFORMATION... I THINK WE SHOULD DO THAT.
WELL, THEN...!

REEEACH

WHAT?! NEVER!

Don't touch me!!!

LET'S SHAKE HANDS AND MAKE UP!

SLAP! OW

FLAIL FLAIL PEEK

NO! IT'S NOTHING!

AM I... INTERRUPTING SOMETHING?

Umm... YOUR CLOTHING HAS GOTTEN QUITE SOILED, SO...

I'M SORRY NOTHING IS AVAILABLE BUT MY OLD GARMENTS...

BUT I THOUGHT YOU MIGHT WISH TO CHANGE INTO THEM.

CRINKLE

WHO, ME?! Really?

SPICA-SAN, IF I MAY.

Panel	Text
	YES, THAT'S WHAT WE'D PLANNED.
	AND WEREN'T YOU GOING TO TAKE A WALK WITH RAIKA-SAMA TODAY, ALICE-SAN?
	TH-THANK YOU VERY MUCH.
	UMM! IMORI... SAN.
	SHALL WE HAVE SOME TEA AFTER YOUR WALK, THEN?
	ABOUT THAT OLD WELL WE PASSED THROUGH LAST NIGHT...
	OH, YES...

THE WEATHER'S SO NICE, ISN'T IT? CLEAR SKIES, CLEAR SKIES!
TWEET
CHEEP...
Yep. IT SURE IS.
This is bad. WHAT SHOULD I TALK ABOUT?
IT'S NOT GOOD TO TALK ABOUT YOURSELF TOO MUCH, RIGHT?
BUT THIS IS MY HOUSE, TWENTY YEARS AGO.
THIS PERSON IS MY MOM, BUT YOUNGER.
WILL I EVER SEE THE MOTHER I REMEMBER AGAIN?

I HAVE TO GET MORE INFORMATION ABOUT THE OUTSIDE WORLD.

WHAT? OH, SORRY!

I KNOW, I KNOW.

I SPACE OUT A LOT WHEN I COME HERE, TOO.

WHAT ARE YOU THINKING ABOUT?

WHEN YOU'RE SURROUNDED BY THE HUGENESS OF THE COSMOS...

ONE PERSON'S WORRIES CAN SEEM SO SMALL AND INSIGNIFICANT, RIGHT?

WHEN I COME OUT HERE, SOMETIMES I IMAGINE MYSELF IN OUTER SPACE.

HUH?

YOU KNOW, THE WORD "COSMOS"... ALSO MEANS "UNIVERSE" AND "ORDER."

WHEN I DO THAT...
A SINGLE PERSON'S LIFE OR DEATH...
IS BUT THE BLINK OF AN EYE IN THE VASTNESS OF THE UNIVERSE.
PLUCK...
EVEN IF I DISAPPEARED FROM THIS UNIVERSE...
IT WOULDN'T BE A BIG DEAL IN THE GRAND SCHEME OF THINGS. THAT'S WHAT I THINK.
YEAH, RIGHT.
HEY, PAPII, WHAT DID YOU BRING ME?
RAIKA...
HMM?

HOP

I'VE BEEN WAITING FOR YOU TO ASK!

I'VE NEVER SEEN ANYTHING LIKE IT.

IT'S OBVIOUSLY A COSMOF, THOUGH.

IT'S NOTHING.

SO, WHAT IS PAPII?

YOU KNOW WHAT? PAPII IS...

AN ALIEN!

THE FOREST, WHERE THE OLD WELL IS...

IT'S CONNECTED TO SOME KIND OF MYSTERIOUS SPACE.

PAPII CAME FROM THAT OLD WELL, TOO.

SINCE LONG AGO...
THIS HILL HAS BEEN A PLACE WHERE THINGS DISAPPEAR AND AP-PEAR.
PAPII IS AN ALIEN THAT CAME OUT OF A WELL?
Alien.
POP
Ah ha ha!
I CAME UP WITH THE IDEA THAT PAPII'S AN ALIEN!
I CAME UP WITH THE NAME "PAPII," TOO!
BUT, YOU KNOW, I DIDN'T EVER THINK A PERSON WOULD COME OUT OF THERE.
YOU KNOW HOW THE STORIES GO IN MANGA, RIGHT?
SUDDENLY, THE HEROINE APPEARS FROM AN-OTHER WORLD AND THEN THE STORY BEGINS--THAT KIND OF THING!
This is just her imagination.
Doppel-gänger Alice, mes-senger from the Under-world?
IT HAPPENED RIGHT BEFORE MY EYES! MOST PEOPLE NEVER GET TO EXPERIENCE SOMETHING LIKE THAT!
THAT'S WHY I'M SO HAPPY TO HAVE MET YOU, ALICE.

YOUR NAME, "ALICE," EVEN SOUNDS LIKE SOMETHING STRAIGHT OUT OF A STORY!
I CAN'T HELP IT. IT FEELS LIKE FATE, SINCE YOU LOOK EXACTLY LIKE ME!
......
OH, I'M SORRY.
I JUST ...
YOU'RE HERE FOR A REASON, AREN'T YOU?
UH...
YOU DON'T HAVE TO TELL ME IF YOU DON'T WANT TO!
I WON'T ASK YOU ANYTHING!
IT'S JUST... PLEASE STAY HERE, JUST A WHILE LONGER.
!
PLEASE BRING SOME EXCITEMENT INTO MY LIFE!

HER ARMS ARE SO THIN.
OKAY, I'LL STAY A LITTLE LONGER.
I'D LIKE TO KNOW MORE ABOUT THIS PLACE...
AND I DON'T HAVE ANYWHERE TO STAY, SO...
GLOMP
THANK YOU... ALICE!
Gah!

SHE SMELLS SO FA-MILIAR.
……………!
I'M SEARCHING FOR MY MOTHER, WHO DISAPPEARED SIX YEARS AGO.
BUT...
IT DOESN'T MATTER WHETHER SHE'S A CHILD OR AN ADULT.
THE PERSON IN FRONT OF MY EYES RIGHT NOW IS...

THE ONE I'VE WANTED FOR ALL THIS TIME TO COME HOME...
THE PERSON I'VE LONGED FOR...
MY MOTHER, AMAKAWA RAIKA.

Chapter 05 Rain

I DON'T LIKE THE TOWN. IT'S SCARY.

FROM THAT DAY ON, EVERYONE IN THE OUTSIDE WORLD ACTED COLD TOWARDS ME.

HEY, ISN'T THAT THE KID?

THE DAMAGE FROM THOSE PESTS...

SPLISH SPLISH SPLISH

HEY, YOU'RE THE **AMAKAWA** GIRL, AREN'T YOU?

WHEN ARE YOUR PARENTS COMING HOME?

HEY, YOU! YOUR STUPID **PETS** DESTROYED MY HOUSE!

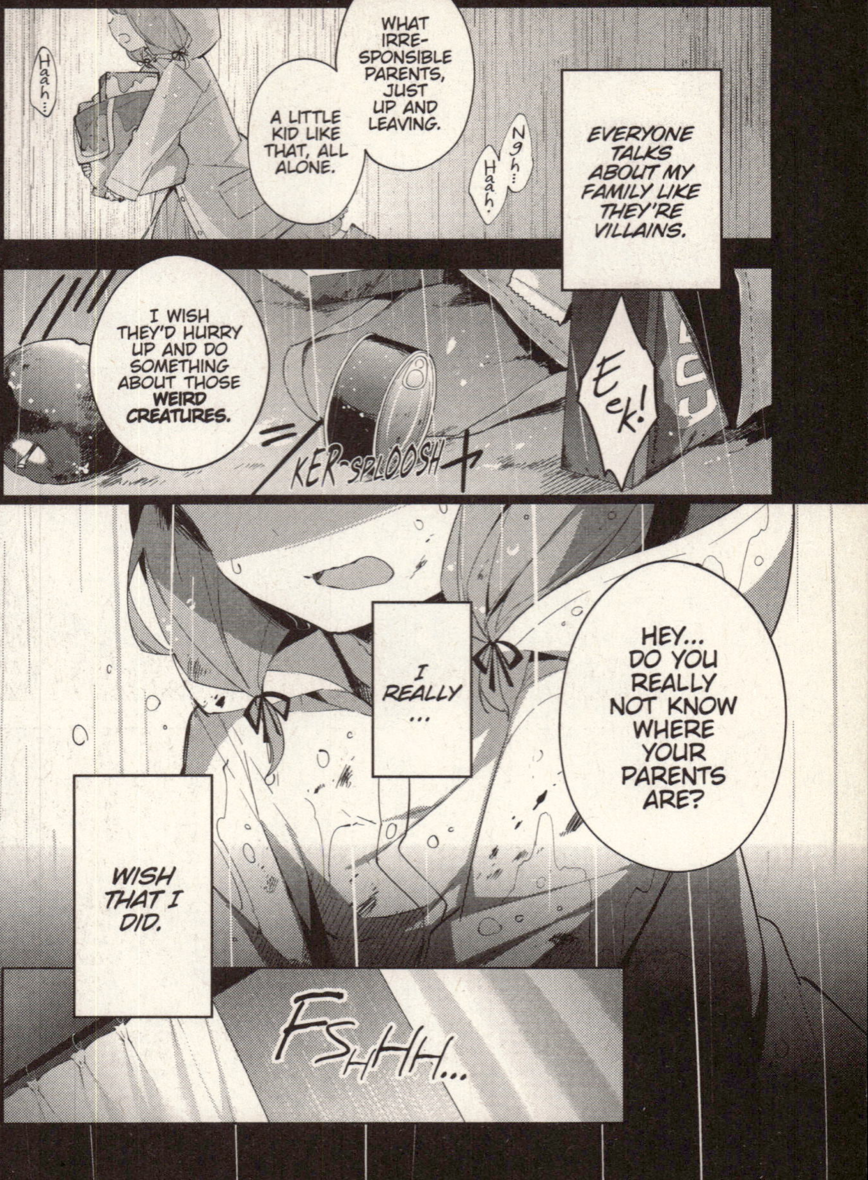
EVERYONE TALKS ABOUT MY FAMILY LIKE THEY'RE VILLAINS.
Ngh... Haah.
WHAT IRRE-SPONSIBLE PARENTS, JUST UP AND LEAVING.
A LITTLE KID LIKE THAT, ALL ALONE.
Haah...
Eek!
KER-SPLOOSH
I WISH THEY'D HURRY UP AND DO SOMETHING ABOUT THOSE WEIRD CREATURES.
HEY... DO YOU REALLY NOT KNOW WHERE YOUR PARENTS ARE?
I REALLY...
WISH THAT I DID.
FSHHH...

I must have fallen asleep.

FS

H
HH
H

Papii hasn't gotten any better. He's been like this ever since we got here.

DRIFT...

It's me, Spica.

KNOCK KNOCK

Come in.

When I was left alone, you were the only one... who stayed with me.

KA-CLUNK...
I KNOW IT'S ONLY THE SECOND DAY SINCE WE ARRIVED...
BUT HAVE YOU FOUND ANY HELPFUL INFORMATION?
Well...
A LITTLE... HEY, I LIKE...
YOUR OUTFIT.
DA
TA-
Ha ha!
I LOVE IT!
MY OTHER CLOTHES STOOD OUT TOO MUCH HERE, YOU KNOW.
RAIKA-DONO EVEN COMPLIMENTED ME, TOO.
Woooow! Isn't that Imori's?!
It looks reeaally good on you! So cuuuute!!!
I SEE.
Isn't that nice?
YOU'VE LOOKED GOOD FROM THE MOMENT I MET YOU.

BLURP...
ACCORDING TO WHAT RAIKA AND IMORI SAID...
THAT OLD WELL WE FELL INTO...
HAS A LEGEND. THINGS GET **SPIRITED AWAY** THROUGH IT.
IT'S A PLACE WHERE THINGS APPEAR AND DIS-APPEAR.
BUT WE WERE THE FIRST ACTUAL PEOPLE TO APPEAR.
SO THEN, IT'S NOT A PLACE THAT PEOPLE FREQUENT.
I WISH WE HAD MORE INFORMA-TION.
LET'S GO INVES-TIGATE LATER.

"So, then... how do you plan to search for your parents, Alice-dono?"

"It's not as though you could inquire about them over here."

"Maybe we should to go into town and ask around?"

"I have a question about your organization, Nix."

"You still want to exterminate the Cosmofs, right?"

"Huh...?"

"The Cosmofs are my family."

"Can you help a member of your enemies' family?"

ISN'T THAT WHAT THE COSMOF THAT BROUGHT US HERE SAID?

"IF YOU BRING BACK AMAKAWA RAIKA, THE COSMOFS WILL STOP RUNNING AMOK."

IN LIGHT OF WHAT'S HAPPENED SO FAR, I'M WILLING TO EXPLORE THAT POSSIBILITY.

AFTER ALL, MY ULTIMATE GOAL IS TO SAVE THE WORLD...

NOT TO EXTERMINATE THE COSMOFS.

I JUST... WANT MY NORMAL LIFE BACK.

I JUST...

"YOU WOULDN'T UNDERSTAND HOW THAT FEELS, WOULD YOU?"

"HOW A PEACEFUL, NORMAL FAMILY..."

"WAS SUDDENLY ONE DAY HATED BY EVERYONE IN THE WORLD."

"HEH."

"I DON'T REALLY UNDERSTAND IT MYSELF."

"I DON'T KNOW MUCH ABOUT THE OUTSIDE WORLD."

SNIP

"BEFORE I GOT TO LEARN VERY MUCH, I DESTROYED EVERYTHING THAT WOULD CONNECT ME TO IT."

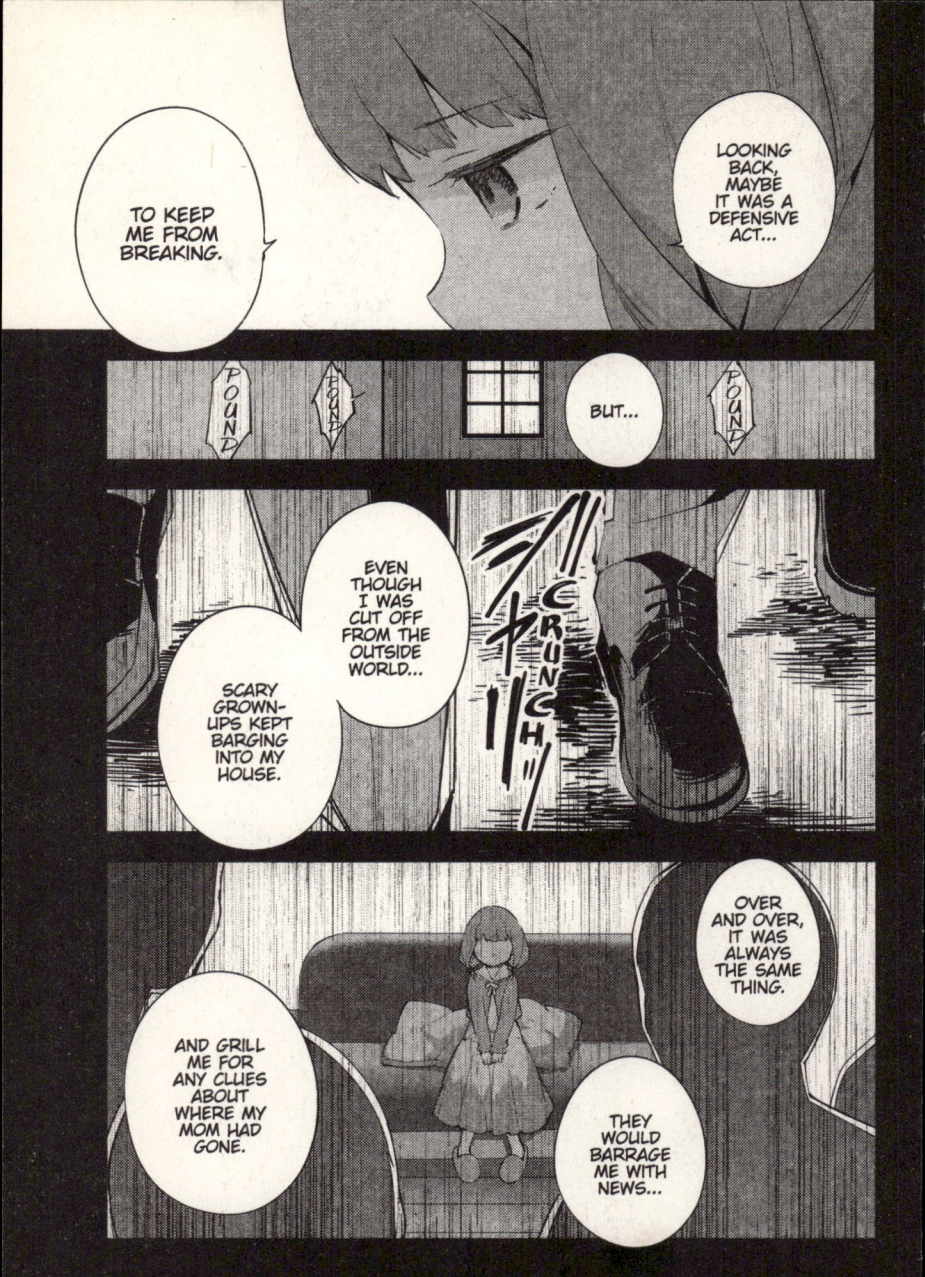

LOOKING BACK, MAYBE IT WAS A DEFENSIVE ACT...
TO KEEP ME FROM BREAKING.
POUND
BUT...
POUND
POUND
CRUNCH
EVEN THOUGH I WAS CUT OFF FROM THE OUTSIDE WORLD...
SCARY GROWN-UPS KEPT BARGING INTO MY HOUSE.
OVER AND OVER, IT WAS ALWAYS THE SAME THING.
THEY WOULD BARRAGE ME WITH NEWS...
AND GRILL ME FOR ANY CLUES ABOUT WHERE MY MOM HAD GONE.

I SOON REALIZED...

THAT I MYSELF WOULD HAVE TO PROTECT...

THIS HOUSE AND ITS MEMORIES FROM DESTRUCTION.

THAT'S WHY...

ALICE?

WHAT'S WRONG? ALL OF A SUDDEN...
LET'S STOP FOR TODAY.
I'M GOING TO HELP WITH DINNER.
I'M SORRY, I GOT OFF-TOPIC.
No. I'M SORRY I MADE YOU RELIVE BAD MEMORIES.
I'LL SEE YOU LATER.
KER-THUNK...

THIS IS THE STARTING POINT OF THE COSMOF RAMPAGE FROM SIX YEARS AGO.

IT MAY BE DIFFICULT TO GET INFO FROM ALICE ABOUT HER MOTHER.

THE COSMOFS FIRST APPEARED TWENTY YEARS AGO... HOWEVER...

THERE ARE NO RECORDS ABOUT WHY OR HOW THEY CAME HERE.

IF THIS IS REALLY THE AMAKAWA RESIDENCE FROM TWENTY YEARS AGO...

THEN THERE'S A GOOD CHANCE THAT I CAN LEARN MORE ABOUT THE RELATIONSHIP BETWEEN THE COSMOFS AND THE AMAKAWA FAMILY.

FS

SHHHH

IT WAS A LUCKY CHANCE THAT WE CAME HERE.

I'LL KEEP OBSERVING HER.

RUSTLE...
FWUMP
I HAD FORGOTTEN... IT WAS LIKE A BAD DREAM.
I'M SO SICK OF THAT HORRIBLE WORLD.
I JUST WANT WHAT I USED TO HAVE.
THE FLOWER GARDEN, FULL OF MEMO-RIES...
MY MOTHER, SMILING...
KIND IMORI...
TEA THAT SMELLS NICE, AND YUMMY TREATS...

"......"

"ALL THOSE THINGS ARE HERE, THOUGH-- RIGHT HERE."

"HEY, PAPII. CAN I JUST STAY HERE FOREVER?"

"I KNOW RAIKA WILL SAY IT'S OKAY."

THAT'S RIGHT.

EVERYTHING...

"I DON'T HAVE TO LOOK FOR THE MOTHER WHO LEFT ME."

"EVERYTHING I'VE WANTED ALL THIS TIME..."

I'LL GO... HELP, TOO.

FSHH...

WHAT AM I THINKING?

CLATTER

SKID...

KER-CHAK

Raika-sama!

RAI...
KA...?

"I apologize for alarming you."

"It seems she overtaxed herself and her condition has deteriorated."

"I must attend to her until the doctor comes..."

"So dinner will be delayed."

"I'll clean up the living room, then."

"Thank you. I apologize for imposing."

TMP...

Chapter 06 Night

RAIKA... IS SOMETHING THE MATTER WITH HER?	ALICE-SAN, ARE YOU RETURNING TO YOUR ROOM, THEN?
	UMM...

YES.

SO...SHE WAS DISCHARGED, RIGHT?

SHE HAD BEEN HOSPITALIZED FOR A LONG TIME... BUT SHE WAS MOVED BACK HERE ABOUT A MONTH AGO.

"THE DOCTOR HAS SAID...

THAT SHE DOESN'T HAVE MUCH MORE TIME."

"SHE WISHES TO SPEND HER FINAL DAYS AT HOME, IN FAMILIAR AND COMFORTING PLACES.

THAT IS WHY SHE WAS "DIS-CHARGED.""

"WHAT...?

SHE HAS BEEN FRAIL FROM BIRTH...

AND HER HEART IS ESPECIALLY WEAK."

""FINAL DAYS"?"

E...
EVERYTHING WILL... BE FINE!
I KNOW RAIKA WILL GET WELL!
SO, DON'T SAY "FINAL DAYS," THAT'S--
ALICE-SAN.
PLEASE DO NOT SPEAK OF SUCH THINGS IN FRONT OF HER.
AFTER ALL, SHE KNOWS BEST ABOUT THE STATE OF HER OWN HEALTH.
....

BZZ
BZZZ
EXCUSE ME.
YES?
I SEE... IS THAT SO?
I WILL HEAD OVER THERE IMMEDIATELY.
Director Yanagi
......
I'M SORRY, BUT I MUST GO AND FETCH THE DOCTOR.
WHAT'S HAPPENED?
THE DOCTOR'S CAR IS STUCK AND CANNOT MOVE.
THE ROADS AROUND HERE ARE BAD, AND THEY WORSEN IN THE RAIN.

MY APOLOGIES, ALICE-SAN, BUT...
MAY I ENTRUST THE HOUSE TO YOU IN MY ABSENCE?
PLEASE STAY BY RAIKA-SAMA'S SIDE IN MY PLACE.
WHY...?
WHY...
DO YOU TRUST ME?
BECAUSE RAIKA-SAMA WISHES IT.

KER-CHAK

I, TOO...

I'M SORRY I SPOKE SO INTENSELY EARLIER.

BELIEVE THAT THERE MUST BE SOME MEANING...

BEHIND WHY YOU BOTH CAME HERE, TO THIS HOUSE.

FSHHH

KER

I MUST BE GOING NOW.

CLUNK...

BEEEP
BEEEP
BEEEP

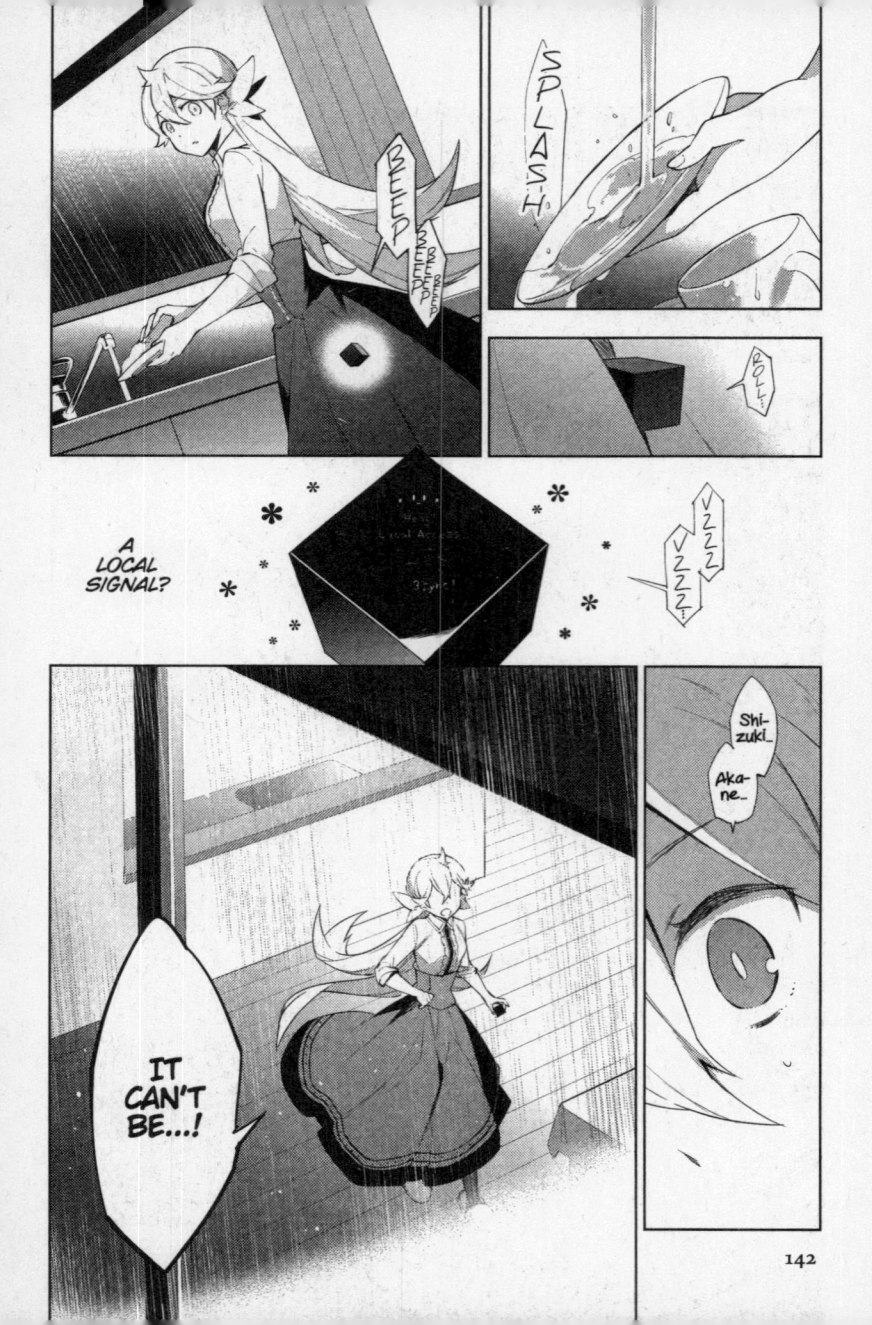

SPLASH

ROLL

A LOCAL SIGNAL?

VZZZT
VZZZT

Shizuki...
Akane...

IT CAN'T BE...!

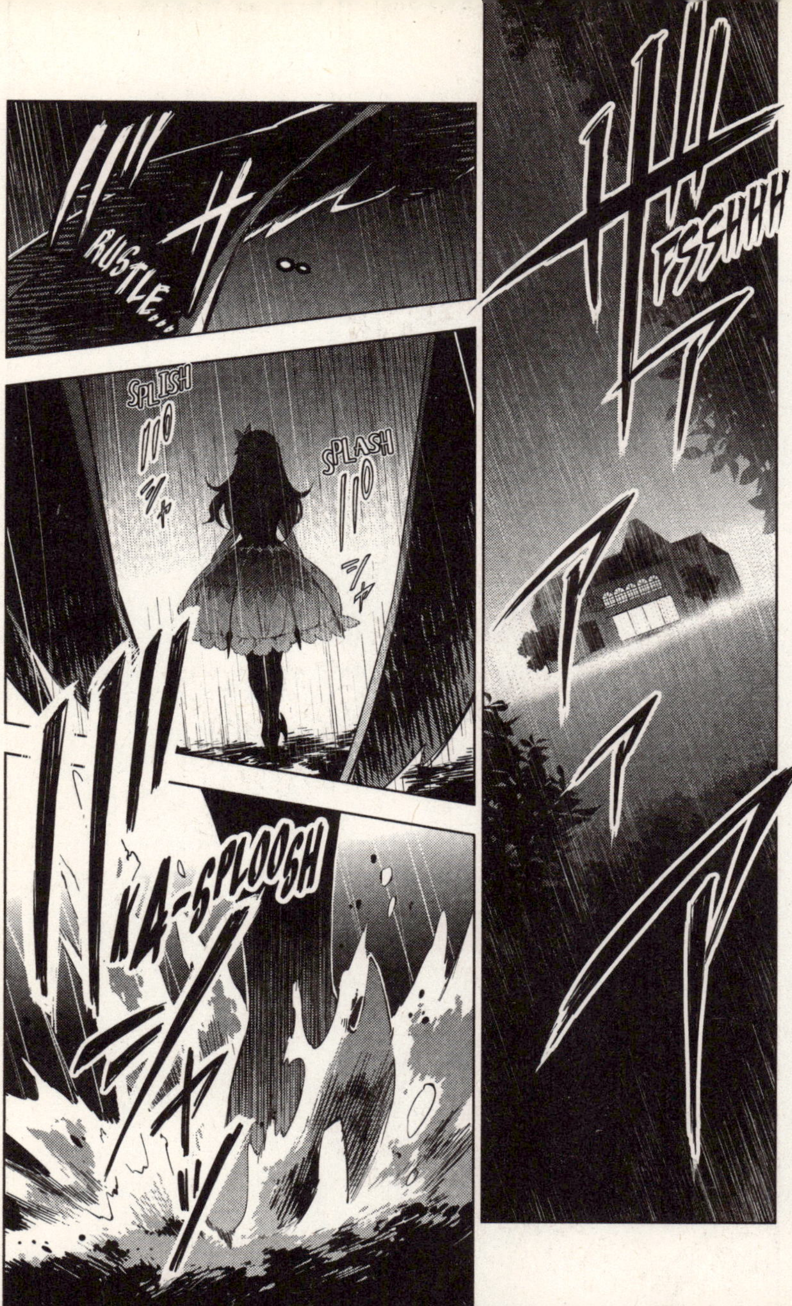
FSSHHH
RUSTLE...
SPLASH
SPLISH
KA-SPLOOSH

RAIKA...

I DIDN'T KNOW THAT MOTHER-SAMA HAD BEEN SO SICK.

I NEVER KNEW ANYTHING.

POIK...

I STILL CAN'T BELIEVE WHAT IMORI SAID.

YOU'RE... WORRIED ABOUT YOUR MOMMY TOO, AREN'T YOU?

THE RAIKA I KNEW WAS ALWAYS HEALTHY AND FULL OF ENERGY.
HEY... WHAT HAPPENED TO RAIKA BACK THEN?
?
FORGET IT.
I...
IT'S MY OWN FAMILY ...
BUT I NEVER KNEW ANY OF THIS.
CLENCH...
DING DONG...

I'M SORRY. WATCH OVER RAIKA FOR ME, OKAY?

KER-CHAK

RUMBLE

WELCOME BA--

IMORI'S BACK? THAT WAS QUICK.

THIS IS THE AMAKAWA RESIDENCE...

ISN'T IT?

DULIN

RUMBLE
RUMBLE

......

MIRA...?

I'M SO GLAD YOU REMEMBER.

GOOD EVENING.

I DRESSED UP, SINCE WE HAVEN'T SEEN EACH OTHER IN A FEW DAYS.

THAT'S RIGHT, I'M MIRA.

DRIP...

WHY... HOW...?

HAVE YOU COME TO ARREST ME?

PLEASE WAIT JUST A MOMENT...

SCUFF...

I'LL GO GET SPICA... RIGHT NOW...

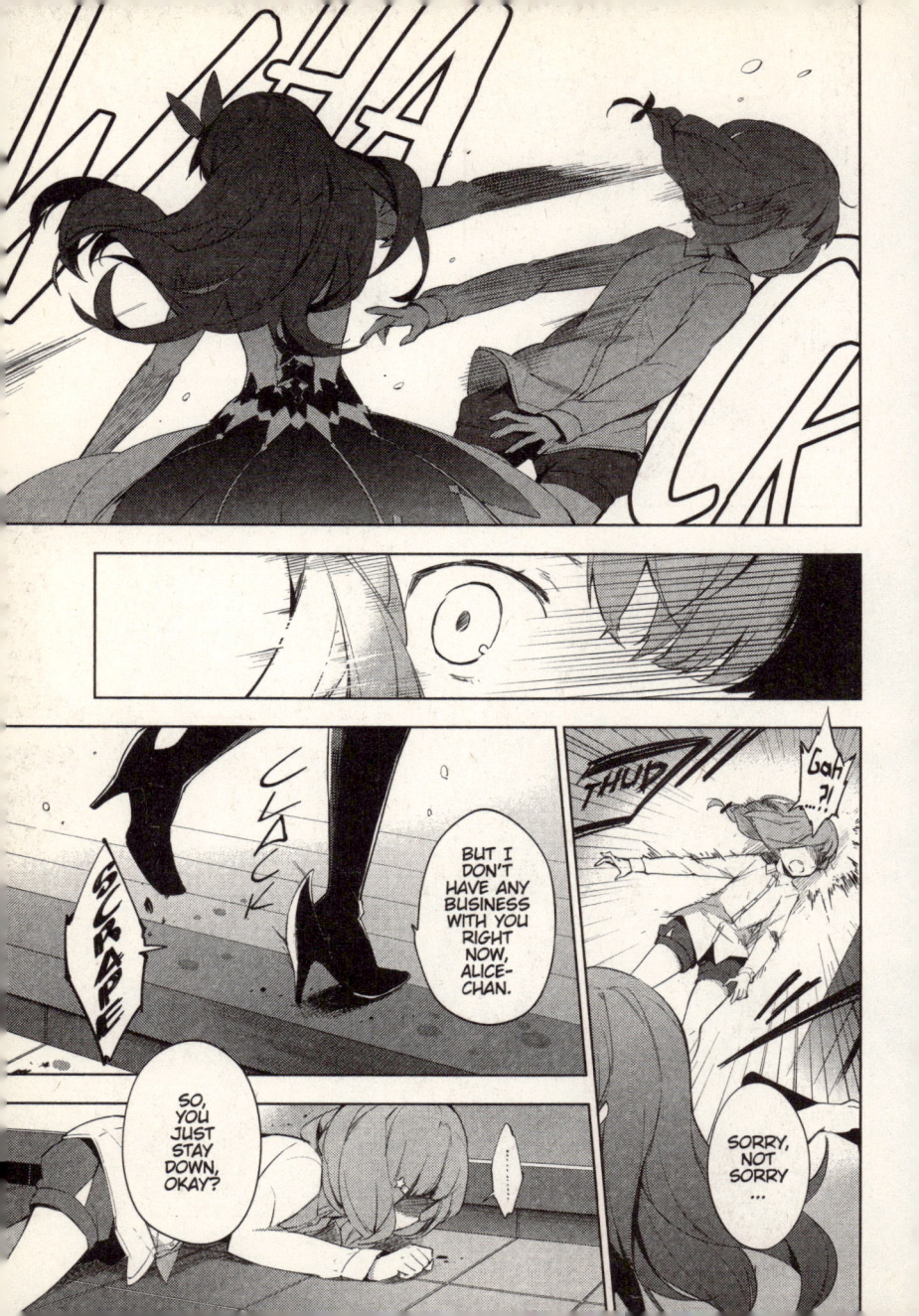

THUD
Gah?!......
CLACK
SCRAPE
BUT I DON'T HAVE ANY BUSINESS WITH YOU RIGHT NOW, ALICE-CHAN.
SORRY, NOT SORRY...
SO, YOU JUST STAY DOWN, OKAY?
......

WH-WHAT ...?!
WHY... NGH!
SHE'S HERE, ISN'T SHE?
THE IN-STIGATOR OF THE COSMOFS' RAMPAGE ...
AMAKAWA RAIKA! I'M HERE FOR *HER.*

......
FSS
HH
H
HH
MIRA ...!
Chapter 07 Transform
CLACK
I'M SO GLAD YOU'RE ALL RIGHT, SPICA.
...!

SHLK
AND DON'T FORGET US!
FLIP
MINIONS 01 AND 02, READY AND WILLING!
AKANE!
SHI-ZUKI!
GRAB
YOU CAN'T JUST BARGE IN HERE! THIS IS...!
WHOOPS!
JUST DON'T MOVE!
NGH...!
Humph...
AREN'T I THE ONE YOU'RE AFTER, MIRA?!

SHIZUKI-CHAN, WHAT IS OUR OBJECTIVE?
TO EXTERMINATE THE COSMOFS!
AKANE-CHAN, WHERE ARE WE RIGHT NOW?
THE AMAKAWA RESIDENCE, TWENTY YEARS IN THE PAST.
CORRECT!
SO, TODAY...
WE'RE HERE TO APPREHEND THE INSTIGATOR AND THE "ORIGINAL" COSMOF.

"INSTIGATOR"...? YOU MEAN...?

EVEN YOU GET IT, DON'T YOU, FLOWERS-FOR-BRAINS?

THAT MUST MEAN THAT PAPII IS THE FIRST COSMOF.

THIS IS THE AMAKAWA RESIDENCE, TWENTY YEARS AGO...

AND THIS IS ALSO THE POINT OF ORIGIN OF THE COSMOFS.

WE COULD TRY TO CONVINCE RAIKA-CHAN...

AND THE ORIGINAL COSMOF TO COOPERATE IN THE NAME OF FUTURE PEACE.

......

SO, THAT'S ONE OPTION. THEN AGAIN...

IF WE KILLED ALL THE AMAKAWAS HERE AND NOW...
WOULDN'T THAT ALSO LEAD TO FUTURE PEACE?
HEE HEE! I KID! I'M JUST KIDDING!
BUT IT REALLY WAS SUR-PRISING, YOU KNOW...
TMP...
TMP...
WHEN WE FOLLOWED YOU AND ENDED UP AT YOUR HOUSE TWENTY YEARS IN THE PAST.
GRIP
I'VE GOTTEN RAIKA AND EVERY-ONE ELSE MIXED UP IN THIS!
......
WHAT SHOULD I DO ...?!

No.

Oh my!

Good evening.

More... guests?

No!

Raika, run!!

Are you Amakawa Raika-chan?

KER-THUNK
MIRA-CHAN, I CAN'T FIND THE PET.
Why are you looking there?
IT'S PROBABLY HIDING IN THE SHADOWS SOMEWHERE. HUNT IT DOWN!
HEY...
WHAT ARE YOU DOING?
THERE ISN'T ANYTHING OF VALUE HERE.
EXCUSE ME?
HEE, HEE! OH, WAIT...
DO YOU THINK WE'RE BURGLARS?

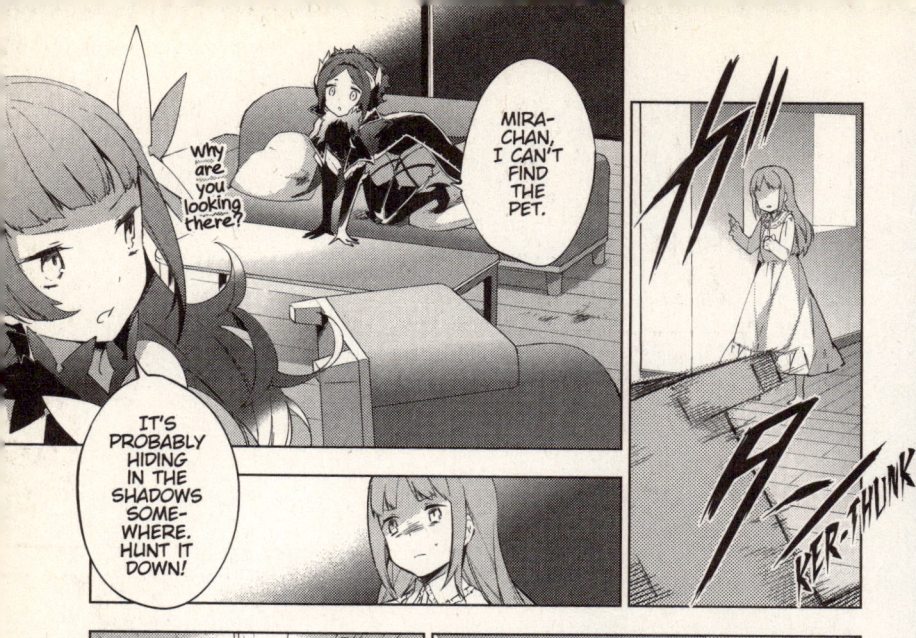

"WE'RE HERE TO CATCH THE BAD GUYS, YOU KNOW."

"LISTEN, DON'T BE SURPRISED, RAIKA-CHAN..."

"......"

"BUT EVERYONE HERE HAS COME FROM THE FUTURE."

"THE FUTURE VERSION OF YOU, AND YOUR FAMILY... ARE GOING TO DO SOMETHING UNBELIEVABLY EVIL."

"I AM...?"

THAT'S RIGHT.
FUTURE YOU IS A HORRIBLE CRIMINAL.
YOU WILL HIDE YOURSELF AWAY FROM THE WORLD.
MEANWHILE, YOUR DANGEROUS PETS WILL OVERRUN THE EARTH.
THEY WILL DESTROY ALMOST EVERY-THING...
AND BRING MISFORTUNE TO COUNTLESS PEOPLE.

RAIKA-CHAN, YOU HAVE A **MYSTERIOUS PET**, DON'T YOU?
IN THE FUTURE, IT'LL TURN INTO A DANGEROUS ANIMAL.
SO, IF YOU COULD JUST BRING IT OVER HERE...
SLIDE...
Ungh...
...?
WHAT'S WRONG...?
......
ARE YOU... SICK?
......
HUMPH.

Ah ha!
IS THIS THE LEGENDARY "AMAKAWA RAIKA"?!
SHE'S JUST A PATHETIC INVALID!
Ha ha!
SNATCH
Ngh.
FWIIP
WELL... THIS WORKS OUT FOR ME.
YOU'RE JUST ANOTHER LITTLE PEST!
I'LL MAKE YOU TALK!

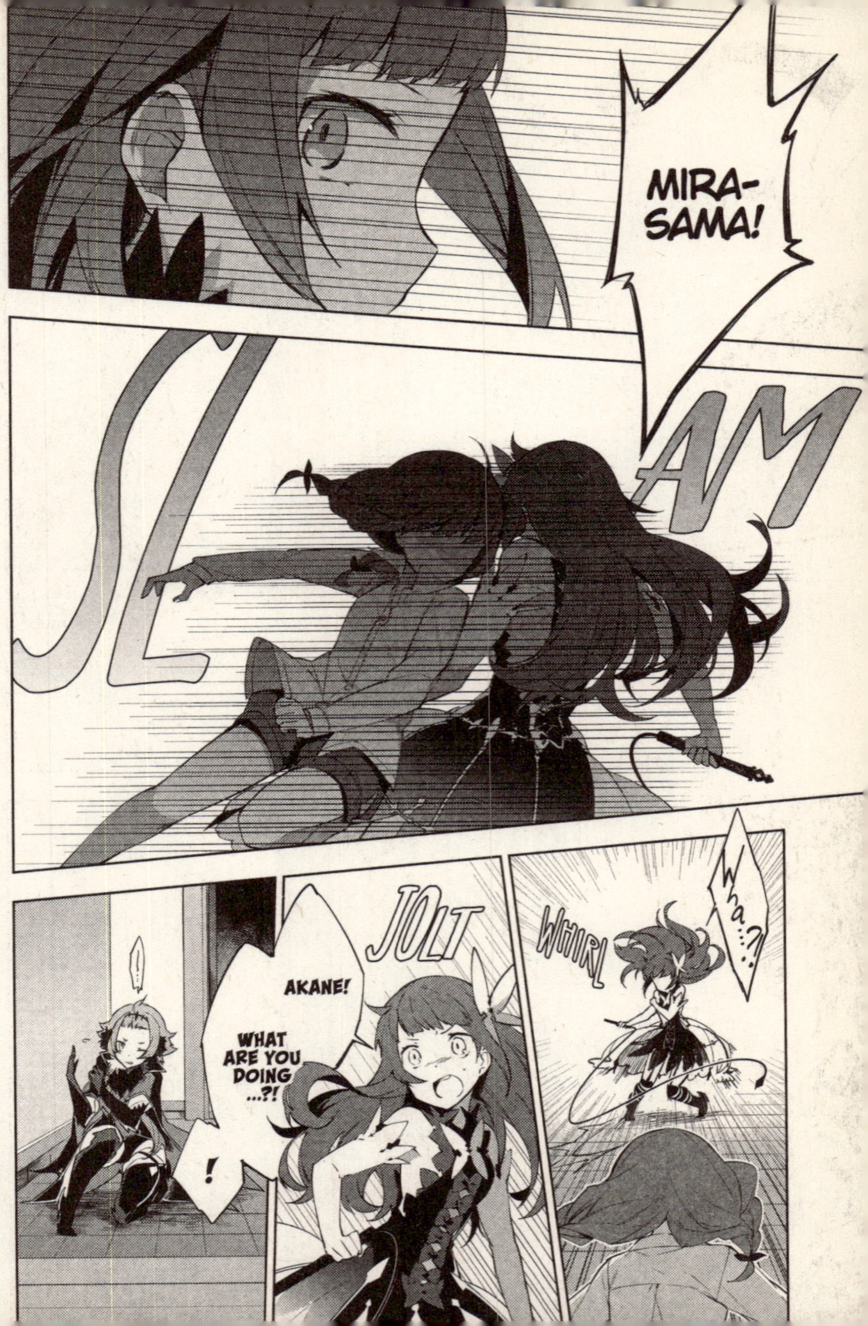
MIRA-SAMA!
SLAM
Wha...?!
WHIRL
JOLT
AKANE!
WHAT ARE YOU DOING ...?!
!
!

FLOAT
FWIP
YOU... CRAZY-POWERED NUISANCE!
KA-SNAP
GET OUT OF MY WAY...
YOU OUTSIDER PEOPLE ARE ALWAYS LIKE THIS!
ALICE-CHAN!
HUH?!

NO ONE TRULY UNDER-STANDS WHAT MY MOTHER DID!
SHF
YOU BARGE INTO MY HOUSE...
YOU JUST ASSUME ALL THE AMAKAWAS ARE BAD!
PA-THWAP
AND JUST REPEAT THE SAME GARBAGE!
HUH? HOW DARE YOU GET MAD AT ME?!
BUT...
I AM ALSO PARTLY TO BLAME FOR LETTING THINGS GET THIS WAY!

SMACK
THWACK
I WAS SO AFRAID OF WHAT WAS GOING ON IN THE OUTSIDE WORLD...
THAT I LOOKED THE OTHER WAY!
IF YOU HADN'T COME, I WOULD HAVE STAYED THAT WAY MY WHOLE LIFE!
THUNK
I TOLD MYSELF THAT MY MOTHER HAD LEFT ME BE-HIND...
WHOOSH
WITH THE COS-MOFS...
THUD
SO THAT I COULD FIND OUT THE TRUTH...
SNAP
BUT THAT WOULDN'T HAVE FIXED ANY-THING!
AND RESTORE MY FAMILY'S GOOD NAME!
!

"I WILL FIND MY FAMILY AND BRING THEM BACK!"

"SO, YOU OUTSIDERS..."

"LEAVE MY FAMILY ALONE!"

"WE WILL... HANDLE THIS OURSELVES!"

CLUNK...
OUT-SIDER ...?
ME?
Transform Invasion
Passcode: **********
unlock
BEEEEEEP!
YOU RUINED MY LIFE AND YOU *DARE* TO CALL *ME* AN OUT-SIDER?
STAGGER
POP
HA HA!
SNAP
CRACK CRACK
YOU'VE GOTTA BE KIDDING ME.
WHY DO YOU THINK...
!
MIRA!

I LET MY BODY BECOME LIKE THIS?!

KA-CRACK

YOU CALL US "OUTSIDERS"?

I'LL TELL YOU, FLOWERS-FOR-BRAINS!

SLASH

THE COSMOFS ...
TOOK EVERY-THING...
AND EVERYONE FROM US! WE'RE ALL ORPHANS!
......
What ...?

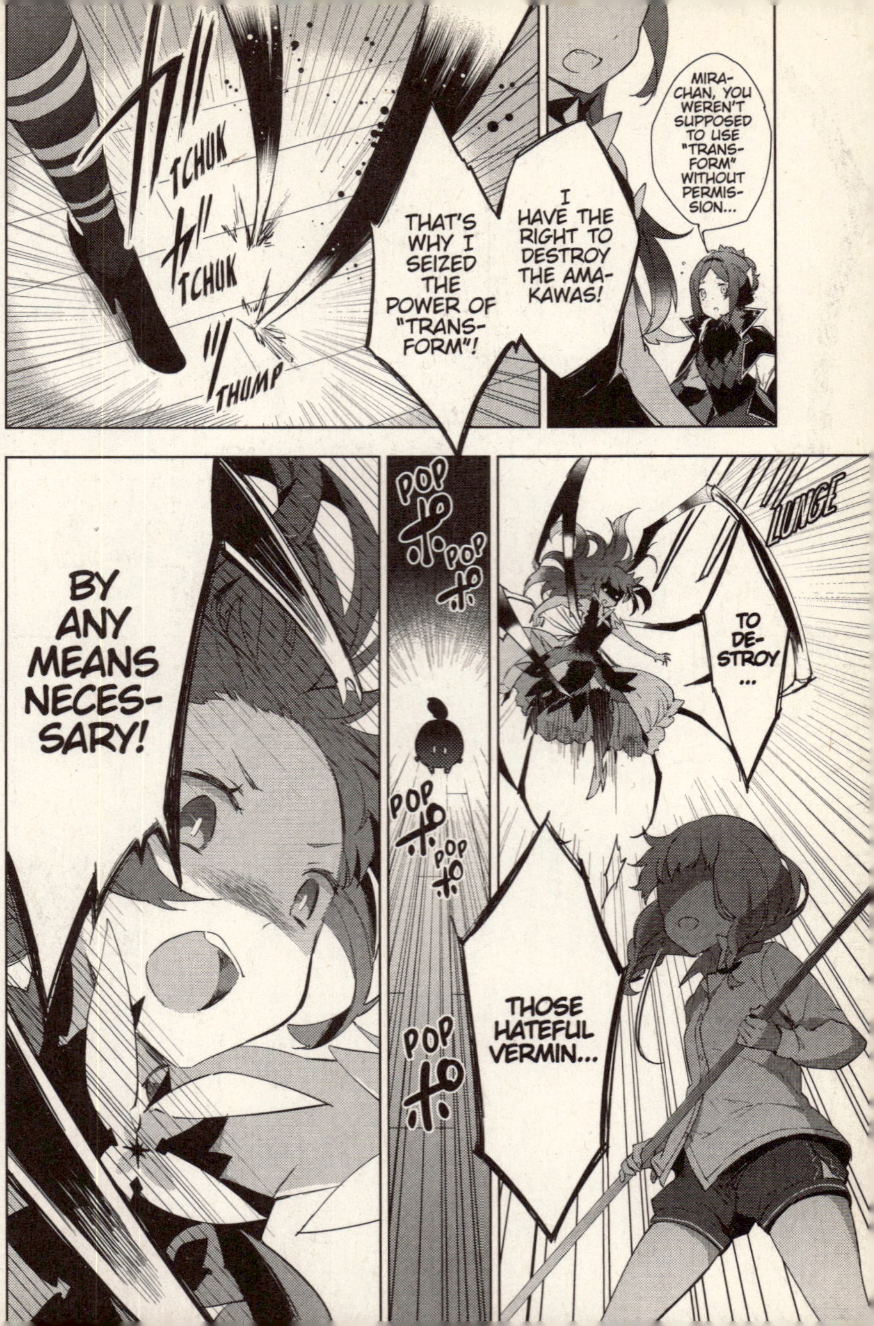
MIRA-CHAN, YOU WEREN'T SUPPOSED TO USE "TRANS-FORM" WITHOUT PERMIS-SION...
I HAVE THE RIGHT TO DESTROY THE AMA-KAWAS!
THAT'S WHY I SEIZED THE POWER OF "TRANS-FORM"!
TCHUK
TCHUK
THUMP
LUNGE
TO DE-STROY...
THOSE HATEFUL VERMIN...
POP
POP
POP
POP
POP
BY ANY MEANS NECES-SARY!

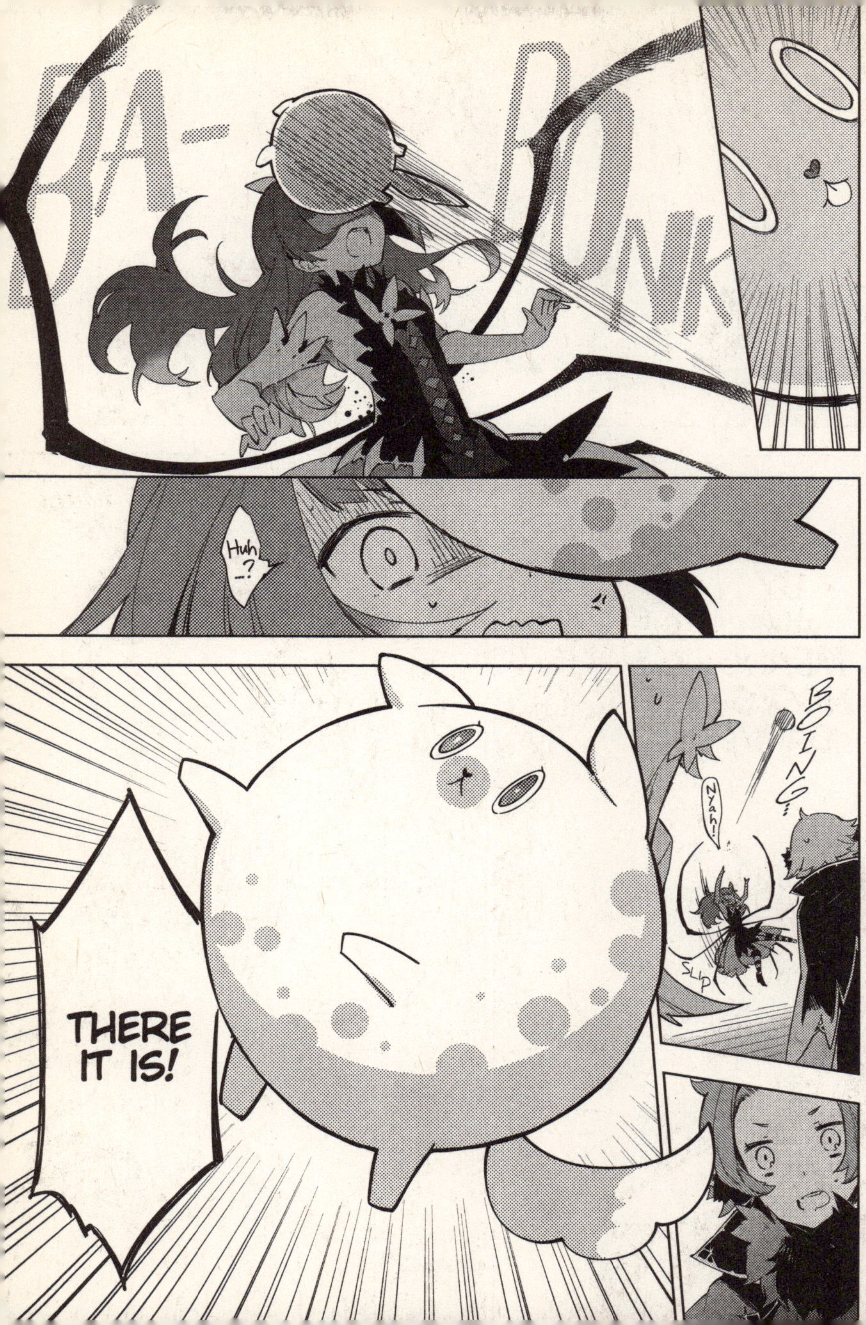
BA-BONK
Huh...?
BOING...
Nyah!
SLIP
THERE IT IS!

CORNER IT!

THE ORIGINAL...

ARGH! CURSED PEST!!

DON'T YOU DARE LET IT GET AWAY!!

PAPII...

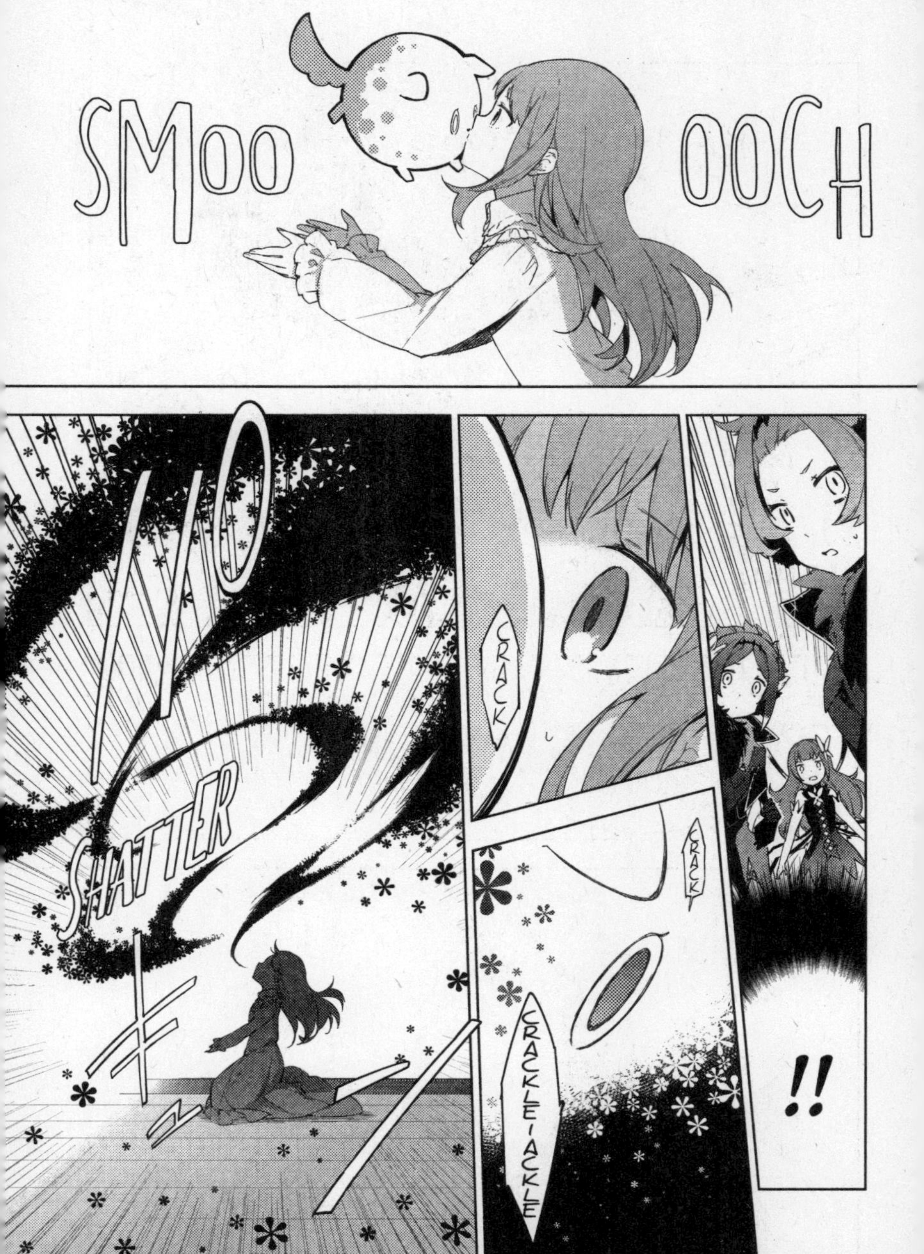
SMOOOOCH
SHATTER
CRACK
CRACK
CRACKLE CRACKLE
!!

BA-DUM

BUIII

UU

ZZZ

SS SS HH HH

RAIKA...?

......

THE ORIGINAL COSMOF...
HAS DISAP-PEARED.
IT'S BEEN EATEN!
SHE ABSORBED IT!
I DIDN'T KNOW ANYTHING ABOUT MY OWN FAMILY.
FROM THAT DAY ON...
THE SECRETS OF THE COSMOFS AND AMAKAWA RAIKA...
THAT I HADN'T KNOWN UNTIL THEN...

BEGAN TO REVEAL THEM- SELVES...

ONE BY ONE.

Cosmo Familia
*
❶

Thank you for using your precious time to read this!

Next time Alice and Raika go to school. Maybe.

This introduction got really long, but this is a story about cute, fluffy alien creatures, so. 🐾🐰
Invasion! A gateway to another dimension! Parasites! Battles with grotesque transformations! Etc, etc!
I'm thinking of letting the story continue along these lines for Volume 2 and beyond.
So, what are the Cosmos, anyway?! To be continued in the next volume.

Hanokage
Thank you so much editor-sama.

SEVEN SEAS ENTERTAINMENT PRESENTS

COSMO✱FAMILIA

story and art by **Hanokage**

VOL. 1

TRANSLATION
Beni Axia Conrad

ADAPTATION
Kim Kindya

LETTERING AND LAYOUT
Carolina Hernández Mendoza

COVER DESIGN
Nicky Lim
George Panella (LOGO)

PROOFREADER
Stephanie Cohen

COSMO FAMILIA VOLUME 1
© Hanokage 2018
First published in 2018 by Houbunsha Co., LTD. Tokyo, Japan.
English translation rights arranged with Houbunsha Co., LTD.

No portion of this book may be reproduced or transmitted in any form without written permission from the copyright holders. This is a work of fiction. Names, characters, places, and incidents are the products of the author's imagination or are used fictitiously. Any resemblance to actual events, locales, or persons, living or dead, is entirely coincidental.

take it from there. If you get lost, just follow the numbered diagram here. It may seem backwards at first, but you'll get the hang of it! Have fun!!